Overdue for Murder

Pecan Bayou, Volume 2

Teresa Trent

Published by Teresa Trent, 2017.

OVERDUE FOR MURDER

First edition. June 22, 2017.

ISBN: 978-1732946866

Written by Teresa Trent.

CHAPTER 1

"You may be disappointed if you fail, but you are doomed if you don't try."
Beverly Sills

"Now don't be nervous. We just need you to stand here behind this counter, and when the red light comes on the camera, talk into it as if you were talking to a neighbor or a friend."

Stan, the station manager of NUTV gently squeezed my arm. His voice was so calming, so friendly. Too bad his efforts didn't seem to have any effect on me.

When Stan asked me to do a weekly fifteen-minute segment for the local cable channel he ran in our small town of Pecan Bayou, Texas, I thought I wouldn't have any trouble at all filling the time. I'd prepared a couple of the columns I had written for the Pecan Bayou Gazette, but when I spoke them aloud to my mirror at home and timed them, I wasn't so sure. I only hoped I had enough material to make it to the time the little red light went off on the camera.

What I was doing today was a vast contrast to the quiet life I had been living in the last eight years. I started out as a single mom and blogger who preferred to stay out of the limelight. Last fall, when Stan and I had both been involved in an investigation run by my aunt and the Pecan Bayou Paranormal Society, he asked me to do this tiny segment on his station.

"Betsy? Are you listening to me?"

"Oh, yes, sorry." It had seemed like such an easy thing to do at the time, but now here I was staring into a blinking red light struggling to talk about freezing dinners ahead of time.

"And 5, 4," Stan counted down the last three numbers on his hand without sound.

"Hi there," I squeaked. "My name is Betsy Livingston, and I am the Happy Hinter!" I heard cheerful music going on behind me making me feel like I should be wearing pearls instead of my dark pink cardigan, white tank and blue jeans. I grasped for the next thing to say as the music started waning. "And today we're going to talk about ... um ... well ..." I cleared my throat and put my hand on the foil-covered dish I had brought with me for a prop. Suddenly I felt my heart beating so fast that I felt a crazy rhythm creeping into my entire nervous system. I simply couldn't go on. What, was I insane trying to do something like this?

I was Betsy Livingston, a single mom who got that way by being rejected by a man who turned out to be nothing but a con. I had worked my way out of it years ago, and today's freeze-up was startling to me. I thought I was past all of this kind of garbage. I thought my meek and mild self died the year I decided to become a writer. There were times when I could actually be quite feisty if I felt I was being run over. At least I thought so. But I guess I hadn't completely transformed myself, and that was why I told Stan I would have to seriously think about whether or not I wanted to be on NUTV.

*****

That afternoon I leaned over the bathtub, my knees hurting on the tiny bathroom tiles. The drain was clogged again, and the thought of calling a plumber was in the back of my mind. This would have been a good time to have a man around the house. Preferably a man in overalls with the name Bob stitched neatly on a white patch. I remembered how my now ex-husband responded to household problems.

"What did you do to it Betsy? We're not made of money, you know."

I knew. Well, I eventually knew. I leaned over the tub again and with great force tried the plunger in the drain. The water bubbled up around the rust-colored rubber stopper, but nothing seemed to be changing. What was that quote about insanity? If you keep doing the same thing over and over and keep getting the same result then you must be insane? Something like that. Inside, a creeping notion kept hitting me that I needed to call up the plumber and pay his $150 to clean the drain. It would be so easy. It would be so expensive.

Sometimes it seemed like life was like that. You could take the easy way out and sacrifice something in the process, or you could go the hard way and find yourself on your knees getting splashed by day-old bath water. Today, I had taken the easy way out and left the TV studio in tears. I felt the shame of my cowardice rising up inside of me. I pushed at the plunger once again with no result. I was even failing at this simple act. As I felt anger building, my thoughts went round and round in self-disgust. As if powered by my own misery, I went all-out and plunged and plunged and plunged, letting out a scream of frustration as I did it.

"Mom, are you alright?" My son came running into the bathroom holding a shiny blue book almost too big for him to carry comfortably.

"Slurrrrrp!" went the drain as the clog cleared.

I pushed back the dark brown bangs that had fallen into my eyes in my moment of exuberance. I had done it, and without help from anyone. Maybe I wasn't so hopeless. "I'm just fine now. Better than fine, I'm great. What are you two guys up to?"

My cousin Danny now stood in the door behind him. He was much taller than Zach, and even though I called him a boy he was only a few years younger than I was.

"We're going to be famous. We're finding a world record to break," Zach said. As I put away the plumber's helper, the boys talked as they went down the hall.

"Look, Danny – this guy did 127 wheelies in one minute. I can do wheelies."

"Not that fast, Zach. Not that fast." My cousin Danny spoke with a slight speech impediment.

"Okay, how about we build the biggest rubber-band ball in the world?"

Danny thought for a moment and then counted on his fingers. "I only got four in my desk at home. How many you got?"

"Mom, how many rubber bands we got?" Zach called out, expecting me to have thousands of spare rubber bands sitting in a shed somewhere waiting for his attempt at an earth-shaking world record.

"Uh, gee Zach, let me look." I put away the plunger and walked down the hall to my office. I pulled out my center desk drawer and started counting. "I see about ten."

"Can we have them?"

"Sure." I pulled the wriggling strings of tan rubber and handed them to him. Zach took one from the bunch, folded it over and then tried to put a second one over it. His little fingers fumbled with stretchy bands.

"Here, let me do it." Danny reached over to grab the rubber bands. His stubby fingers couldn't even get a start on it.

"You guys," I sighed. "Let me show you how to do this." Most boys never have to put up a ponytail with a hair fastener the way a girl would have. Here they were ready to break a world record and couldn't even manipulate the rubber bands. I twisted and turned the tiny piece of rubber until we had a lopsided ball.

"Cool, Mom. We only have to get it to a little over six feet seven inches."

"How big?"

"That's what the guy in the world record book did."

"Zachary, do you know how many rubber bands that would take?"

"I don't know, five bags?"

"Try hundreds of bags – and where do you find a rubber band big enough to stretch six feet?"

"Mr. Simmons' store?" asked Danny. Mr. Simmons' store was our local hardware store downtown. Mr. Simmons would get pretty excited at the thought of selling a giant rubber band.

"Sorry, guys. This plan isn't going to work."

"Aw, Mom. We just have to break a world record. Could we at least try?"

"Try?" I ran my fingers through my straight brown hair. Being the only parent in the house had its days. Today we had Danny over while my aunt was out doing some shopping and having some respite time. Danny and Zach could cook up some big trouble when they wanted to.

"I guess you can try," I said, "but there has to be something that is easier and less expensive than collecting thousands of rubber bands."

The boys settled back onto the floor and opened the world record book. Zach slurped at the straw sticking out of his little red juice box. Danny carefully started turning the pages of the reflective blue world record book. He pointed to a picture of a man with his tongue sticking straight out. "Cool guy," he said with great reverence. "Look Betsy, he's got an earring in his tongue."

"Cooool, he has the record for the most piercings," Zach stroked his chin in thought. "Nope, too painful."

For both of us, I thought. Why do kids always want to do something to make them famous? What is the force that makes us all want to shine just a little brighter than everyone else in the room?

The phone rang next to me. Pecan Bayou Gazette came up on the caller ID.

"Betsy, got a little job for ya," Rocky Whitson, the editor of the paper, crackled on the other end. He always reminded me of sort of a hip grandpa type. He was in his sixties with pale gray hair in the process of going white. Being a single, handsome man over fifty in a town full of divorcees and widows, he had his share of dinner invitations. Although flattered by the attention, he was busy managing our small-town, once-a-week paper, which included only one full-time reporter, who spent most of his time doing sports. Rocky did the rest of the reporting, classified ads and all of the other general jobs. He also had a couple of local bloggers writing weekly columns. I was already writing for my blog five days a week, so having it published in the local paper wasn't any increase in my workload, just more money. With the unpredictable fate of print journalism, Rocky had created a Pecan Bayou Gazette online that he updated daily. The other blog featured in the Gazette covered fashion and style and was written by Vanessa Markham, the wife of the sports reporter. Rocky said he eventually wanted to include blogs about gardening, home repair, politics, religion and whatever else he could find locally.

"Can you cook?"

"Uh, yeah. I do write a helpful hints column and have included tips for cooking shortcuts."

"Right, but can you cook?"

I was a little insulted by that. Of course I could cook. Okay, only cooking for two, and we did often partake in grocery-store precooked meals, but still, I cooked.

"Yes, I cook all the time. That's how we stay alive."

"Good, glad to know it," he chuckled. "The mall is puttin' together its first annual Creative Cooks Day, and I signed you up for it. You and Peter's wife, Vanessa, will be representing the newspaper. This is a way for us to increase visibility and maybe sell some more print subscriptions."

"Creative Cooks? What does that mean exactly?"

"Oh, you know, all that Betty Crocker stuff about frosted pine cones and stacking cake balls into little bitty trees. Whatever it is all you women do with that stuff." I think he had an image in his mind of the secret language of women. Somehow in that world we were elevated to a more aesthetically pleasing existence where we created all things stylish. Unfortunately, it seemed no one had ever sent me the official codebook.

"I don't know, Rocky. This is starting to sound like a little more like art than cooking."

"Well, it is "Creative Cooks," and you're a creative gal. You can do it. Listen, I was talking to Pattie at PattieCake's when I was down getting my donut this morning, and she said she is going to make a giant cupcake tower with eight layers and one of her special cakes on top. Just think up something like that, and remember you're representing the paper."

No pressure. I gulped. I had thrown together a beef stew and lopsided birthday cake, but cupcake towers?

"I'm not a cake decorator, Rocky."

"Sure you are. Let your Martha Stewart flag fly, girl. You write all of this stuff about better ways to do things, so I know you can figure out a better way to bake a cake, right? Haven't you made cakes for your son or for your husband's birthday?" He stopped cold, realizing the mistake he had made. My husband hadn't been around for me to make a cake in the last eight years. I made my living giving other people tips to make their lives easier, and I was pretty good at it. If somebody asked me for a tip on having a fulfilling love life? Call Dr. Phil. That was way out of my league.

"So think on it, Betsy. The contest is in a week at the mall. I'll have all the signs for your table – oh, and bring some of those extra books you got. Maybe you'll sell one of 'em, for once." Rocky hung up.

Ping. That hurt. My book, *The Happy Hinter*, hadn't really taken off in the literary world. It was published locally and distributed in the metropolitan areas of Texas, but that was last year. This year my publisher was spending more time pushing some book about the frogs of Texas. It was a good thing I had the column to write for the Pecan Bayou Gazette and was attempting to film the weekly segment for Stanley at NUTV. Between all of that I had enough paychecks rolling in to support both me and my son. I also did talks for various local groups and silly stuff like this. What kind of cake could I possibly bake?

"Betsy?" My Aunt Maggie was at the back door. She opened the squeaking screen and walked in pulling a sheer scarf off of her freshly teased and sprayed hair.

"Ruby Green says hello." Maggie had just left her weekly haunt, "The Best Little Hair House in Texas." There was more breaking news going on down there than Rocky could ever hope for. If he had any brains he'd plant a reporter at the salon who could cut hair. Maggie heard it all, and thankfully, she brought it back to me. "Anything going on?" I asked.

"Well, heard about one affair, and Ms. Gibbs has been dressing with the blinds up again."

"Something to that," I said as reached for a dusty cookbook, turning the pages to the cake section. I leafed through sumptuous pictures of the kind of birthday cakes you could only dream of on an empty stomach.

"Aunt Maggie, have you ever made one of these fancy cakes?"

"Like what? Like what you see at the grocery?" Maggie's voice rose at the end, exaggerating her Texas accent.

I propped up the book for her to see a cake titled "Undersea Fantasy," which featured crabs, turtles and dolphins all crafted out of what looked like marshmallows and licorice strings. She peered at it, adjusting her bifocals on her nose as I explained to her what Rocky had asked me to do for Creative Cooks Day.

"Gee, Betsy. I'm thinkin' you're in over your head this time. I remember when you tried to make Danny that smiley face cake. The black icing you used on the grin ran down the side and it about scared him to death. Surprised he made it to his next birthday without counselin'."

I scratched my head. "Oh, yeah. I forgot about that, no wonder on the video all the kids were screaming."

"Sure, and then there was the time you tried to make Judd that cake and forgot to put the eggs in."

"I should have caught that."

"Yeah, we had to put candles on a box of honey buns that day. You got a track record for bad baking, baby girl."

Zach and Danny ran into the kitchen. "Mama," Danny said. "We're going to break the world record."

"What world record?" Maggie asked.

"All of them!" Danny answered.

"We're still figuring out what incredible thing we're going to do, Aunt Maggie, so I'm glad you got your hair done." Zach stretched out his arms, imagining his future paparazzi. "There will probably be hundreds of reporters out on the lawn after we do it."

"Thanks for the warning," she smiled.

I paged through the glossy photos in the cookbook. There were cakes that looked like circuses, swimming pools, insects, hats, cartoon characters. I started having a case of baking terror. "You know, Aunt Maggie. I could always drive into Houston and buy something and bring it back. They'll never know."

"You'll know."

I sighed.

"You could make a cake out of rubber bands," suggested Zach.

I nodded. "That's original, but not too tasty." I turned the page and spotted the cake labeled "Beginner's Crocodile Cake." How kind of them to have a cake that was supposed to be easy enough for people like me. I grabbed a pen and started writing down the ingredients I would need. Surely I could stir up some green frosting and turn it into something.

CHAPTER 2

That evening as I checked my email, I had a message from "weatherguy," Leo Fitzpatrick. We had met last October while I had been helping my aunt do her paranormal ghost hunt out at the abandoned tuberculosis hospital on the edge of town. For a while I wasn't sure if I could trust him, especially when he became a suspect in the murder of my ex-husband's partner, Oliver Canfield. He seemed to keep showing up in the wrong place at the wrong time, but in the end he turned out to be a pretty decent guy. It also didn't hurt he was six feet tall and the handsomest man I had met since my husband.

Now I was embarking on the rest of my life, and that included beginning to date. Leo Fitzpatrick was a part of this. Since our finding each other in a pretty dark and scary place, we had spoken on the telephone and emailed, and he had come back to Pecan Bayou a couple of times, staying at the Sinclair Arms, our local hotel. Returning the favor, Zach and I visited him and his nephew, Tyler, in Dallas, and we also stayed at a hotel. Each time we went out it was either with the boys or for a few hours while the boys stayed with a babysitter. Having a long-distance relationship worked for me because even though I really wanted to date again, something kept holding me back.

My time with Barry and the trust he betrayed changed my attitude toward love and marriage. Why couldn't men wear white and black hats to make it easier to tell the good guys from the bad? It would make it so much simpler for all of us in the trenches. I read Fitzpatrick's email.

Dear Betsy,

There is a jazz festival in Dallas next month, and I would love to have you come and visit. Could your dad babysit? Tyler will be at a weekend grief support camp for children who have lost a parent. I miss her too, but they don't have one of those for brothers.

Fitz

I was touched by his honesty. Tyler was a sperm-donor baby, so when his sister took her own life, Leo stepped up to be a combination uncle and father to her son. Reading through his message, I could surmise that he wanted to spend the weekend with me and that he wanted our get-together to be without either his son or mine. Up until this time, the physical side of our relationship had been pretty close to platonic. Taking the boys out of the equation changed things. As long as it felt like we were on a "playdate," I felt perfectly safe. If Fitzpatrick even tried to come near me, Zach would squeeze in between us with some sort of need. Without my fifty-pound protector there, things would be different, and I felt a mixture of terror and delight over the thought of it.

Maybe I could just drive over for the day and make my exit before nightfall. I could make something up, like I have to teach Sunday School or help with a science project that was due on Monday. I tapped my fingers on the keyboard for a moment and then hit reply.

Dear Leo,

Sounds great, but let me check my schedule.

Betsy

That was easy. I didn't say no, but I didn't exactly rush into his arms – and oh how nice that would be. I just needed a little more time to think this out. According to his email, I had several weeks. I had to admit it was time to make some changes in my life, but I also needed to make sure they were changes that would be good for me and Zach. After Barry, I wasn't sure about my own judgment of men, but also having a man like my father in my life, I knew they weren't all bad. Some of them were downright pleasant to be around.

On Sunday afternoon I decided to tackle my first attempt at the crocodile cake. I propped the cookbook open on the counter and looked at an adorable picture of a little bitty crocodile in a bed of raffia straw. It would be so simple. I would bake a couple of cakes in Bundt cake pans. From there I would cut the Bundt cake in three equal pieces and then take one of those pieces and cut it in half sideways. Then I would arrange the three equal pieces to look kind of like a snake. Then take one of the cut halves and make the tail and take the other and cut it into four pieces to make the feet. So easy. It was kind of like sewing with food.

I measured, stirred and poured a box of chocolate cake mix into my Bundt pan and put it into the oven. I needed malted milk balls, a large marshmallow, gummy spearmint leaves, green gumdrops and white yogurt-covered pretzels. The marshmallow, cut in half, would be the eyes, with malted milk balls for the pupils. The spearmint leaves went on his feet for claws, and green gumdrops went on his back for whatever those bump things are on dragons. The yogurt-covered pretzels would be stuck in the head section along where the mouth would be, to look like teeth. For his slimy scaly skin, I would tint some white icing green. I had some multicolored fruit snacks that I could substitute for gumdrops and some real pretzels to make the teeth on my practice crocodile.

As I scoured the cabinets for malted milk balls, Zach came running in with his book of world records. His small frame was swallowed up by a Houston Astros T-shirt he got when my dad took him to an Astros game last year. Zach had been struggling with Little League, and my dad thought it would be a good idea for him to see what baseball was like on a professional level. Zach took it all in, including the overpriced souvenir stand.

"Hey Mom, how long would you say I could go without sleeping?"

"Well, when you were a baby I think you might have been working on that world record." I closed one cupboard door and opened another, still in search. He stood still, waiting for my attention. "Okay, what's the record?" I asked.

"I don't know. It's not in here anywhere. Why is that?" he asked.

"Maybe because if you go without sleep, you die. It's not healthy." I took down the baking powder, now looking to see if the malted milk balls were in the back of the cabinet.

"How do you know that?" he said, looking at me as if I might be making this stuff up.

"I just do. You're a growing boy, and you need all the sleep you can get. What's another record you could break?"

He sat down at the kitchen table and leafed through the pages. "Uh, I could stack the most Legos. Umm, it looks like this guy stacked twenty-one Legos in fifteen seconds."

My hand landed on a crunchy cellophane bag. I had found them at last. The malted milk balls had probably been up there since last Christmas, but they would work for a practice cake. If I hadn't found them I was going to have to use salad olives instead. This would be much more pleasing to the palate.

"That sounds pretty good, Zach. Why don't you go practice?"

He slammed the book shut with a loud pop and ran out of the room again. Life is pretty exciting when you go from adventure to adventure, I thought. The buzzer on the stove went off, and I busied myself preparing the cake to transform into a crocodile. I carefully cut each piece as per the instructions and then angled them just so to make the little crocodile's body. I felt pretty good as I put the frosting over the S-shaped cake. I started sticking the gummy fruit snacks on the back when all of a sudden the cake split. There was a noticeable crack where the sections should have met. Chocolate brown came gaping up between the green icing, making it look like some sort of ghastly roadkill. This would never do. I tried sticking a little icing in between, but still the cracks appeared. How could I make it look like a cute little crocodile when it was starting to look like it had been run over by a pickup truck? I tried attaching toothpicks to it, but by the end of my handling, the delicate cake looked like a sad pile of sod. I had finally made something worse than the smiley face cake. An exploding brown worm.

I looked at my now icing-spattered cake cookbook. There were cakes in there that would bring Rachael Ray to tears. There had to be cake design tips that the Happy Hinter needed to add to her portfolio. I knew just who to ask about this, and that was my friend Pattie at PattieCake's Bakery. If anyone could make a crocodile cake, it was Pattie. If anyone could make a cake stick together, it was also Pattie.

CHAPTER 3

The next day, with my slightly sticky cookbook under my arm, I entered the shop on Main Street with the pink-striped canopy. PattieCake's had been in business for about five years, and during that time I had seen the number of patrons gradually increase year by year. Today, as I walked in, there was a line of people at the counter taking home boxes of cupcakes, donuts, brownies and all those things diet doctors warn against. The smell of fresh yeasty dough, melted butter and that rich aroma of something sweet coming out of the oven hit me and washed over my senses like a warm blanket.

I could see Pattie up at the counter, her long brown hair pulled back in a ponytail. She wore a pink-striped apron covered with splotches of flour and a little bit of blue icing near the midsection. Pattie wasn't overweight, but she wasn't skinny either. I don't know if I would feel comfortable visiting a bakery with a rail-thin baker.

She was in her early thirties and had been a year ahead of me in school. For as long as I could remember, she had been baking. Her mom was a cafeteria lady at our elementary school, and that was probably where Pattie started with her culinary artistry. Her father had been in and out of trouble for years and still lived in a trailer outside of town. Pattie worked during the day and lived with her retired mother. After years of working in a kitchen, her mom had no interest in more long days on her feet.

The bakery that had formerly been named Shorty's Donuts was put up for sale by Shorty's children when he passed away. They wanted to sell the business fast, and Pattie mortgaged her mother's house to qualify for the loan. With that much at stake, Pattie proved to be a savvy businesswoman. She went to the junior college in Andersonville to learn about running an efficient and successful enterprise and brought what she learned home to the bakery.

Between her father's troubles and looking after her mother, Pattie hadn't had much time for a man in her life. She dated a few guys off and on, but none of them worked out. Pattie hadn't ever been a part of the popular crowd in school, probably because her mother was that nice lady in a hairnet scooping mashed potatoes in the cafeteria. She had been taller than most of the girls growing up. My friendship with Pattie started after high school as we both struggled with the men in our lives. I really liked her. And even though we were only acquaintances in school, she had always been nice to me. Pattie was one of those people that no matter what life threw at her, she would face it and move on.

Pattie flashed her friendly smile my way as she bagged up a bear claw. In spite of the crowd drooling at her counter, she still knew I was here. I so hoped she would have some time to help me with my crocodile cake. I looked at the line. There were only two people in front of me now.

I realized I was standing behind our town librarian, Martha Hoffman. Martha was in her forties and was wearing a navy blue blazer that covered her ample behind over a navy floral skirt and flat, efficient shoes. Next to her was Vanessa Markham, the other blogger from the paper. She was beautiful in a way that was a bit different from the standard appearances of the women in Pecan Bayou. Her blonde hair had multiple golden tones streaked into it, and today over her slim frame she wore an outfit consisting of a tan cotton blouse, tan pants and tan three-inch heels. She accented the tan combination with a large gold chain necklace, gold earrings and sunglasses that I could pretty well bet hadn't been bought at the corner drug store.

She was stunning, at least when it came to appearances. Rocky had me proofread her column one time. She had written that the new Gucci bag was ideal and that wearing it to any occasion would make you ideal for any occasion. Until then I had no idea Rocky had been cleaning up her weekly contribution to the paper.

"Her writing style is the worst product of the public school system I have ever seen," Rocky said to me that day. "But the content she turns out is right on target for women's fashion. This is the kind of stuff I could never write." The final product was very popular among the Pecan Bayou readers. Having our very own fashion guru was pretty big-city for our little town.

Vanessa Markham was pointing to a tray of loaded German chocolate cupcakes that Pattie quickly scooped into a pink-striped box and topped them with wax paper. The librarian pointed to a tray of Napoleons for her box.

Martha held her rounded hands together in front of her. "So, Pattie, I know I can count on you to come to my Authors Night. You're such a genius with baking. I know I can't go but a few days without coming back here for more of your delicious goodies. Your new cookbook will be a great addition to our evening. Please consider being a part of it. Vanessa here is going to talk about her incredible chick-lit book. Her book got picked up by the Houston Stars publishing company, and distribution is about to expand outside of Texas."

Vanessa Markham broke off a piece of Napoleon that Martha offered her, using her red-lacquered fingernail to slide it between her lips. "Yes, I'm very excited. Of course my pen name is Vanessa Scarlett. Doesn't that sound so much more exciting than Markham? Well, that and Peter is already an established writer, so I went with Scarlett."

Pattie smiled softly. "I'm so flattered you would even ask me. We just printed out our cookbook to sell here at the store. I'm not exactly published, you know."

Martha Hoffman held her pink-striped box to the blazer covering her ample bosom. "Yes, we know, but you have to admit you have something here." She waved her hand across the packed display case of baked goods.

"Well, thank you," said Pattie. She glanced over in my direction, and then what came close to an evil smile came across her face. "But as long as you are scouting out authors, we have another standing right here with us."

"Who's that?" Martha said, pushing her glasses up with her free hand and glancing around the bakery.

"Why, Betsy here. Her book has actually been published by a real publisher."

"Betsy?" Both women turned around and focused their eyes on me. I waved meekly, still holding on to my sticky cookbook.

"Hi," I said. "I'm Betsy Livingston."

"Hello," said the little librarian. "You've written a book?"

"It was published a couple of years ago. It's a helpful hints book. I write the Happy Hinter column in the newspaper."

Vanessa Markham uttered a gasp in recognition of me. "Oh yes! We haven't formally met. You're the other blogger at the paper."

"Right." I nodded.

"And what's your book called?" Martha asked, shaking her head as if I was just another child trying to check out books without a library card.

"*The Happy Hinter*, same name as the column," I answered, almost apologizing for the lack of creativity in titling my book.

"I don't recall us having anything by that name at the library," Martha Hoffman stated, as if I was probably mistaken about being published because it didn't exist on her shelves.

"Probably not. It was published by a small press. I've only sold about 500 copies so far. Really, I'm sure your evening is already full, so you don't need to add me to your author list."

Pattie scowled. "Betsy, you have a great book, and if I deserve to be there, then so do you. Isn't that so, Martha?"

Martha bit her lower lip as if she had just been outmaneuvered in a chess game.

"Yes, I suppose we could add her to the end of the program. I'm sure your presentation would be fairly short, Miss Linson."

"It's Livingston," I corrected her.

"Martha, that's the deal then. I don't speak unless Betsy gets to speak, too."

Martha looked at her watch. "I have to get back. Well, I guess I'll get two for one today," she said, trying to sound cheerful about her new speaker but not really making it work. The two ladies both rushed a goodbye and headed out the door.

"First thing," I said to Pattie. "I need a box of donuts for the Pecan Bayou Police Department."

"Always glad to serve our men in blue," Pattie said, unfolding another pink-striped box. "Getting out of a parking ticket?"

"With my dad on the force, any parking ticket I get will be paid on time, in full and with a great deal of harassment from Lieutenant Judd Kelsey, super cop."

Pattie laughed. "I thought my old man was bad with all his troubles."

I knew her dad had been in and out of rehab several times in the last twenty years. My dad had probably been the one to arrest him on some of his many charges.

"It's still good, though. You know, that you can talk to him. You and your dad have something special."

"Yeah, well, that's what I'm on my way to do today. That guy I've been seeing from Dallas wants me to spend a weekend with him ... alone."

A look of acknowledgment came into Pattie's eyes. "Oh, I get it. What do you have to ask your dad for? Last time I checked you were a grown woman – with a child, no less."

"I'm not asking him for permission," I said. "I'm asking him what he thinks about it."

"Wow, you and your dad really are cool," Pattie said. "You want my opinion?"

"Sure." I said.

"I think you should go for it. You know, you're only young once, and guys like that don't come along every day. He's single, he's handsome, he isn't a drunk or a druggie, he's employed. Sounds perfect to me – better yet, give him my number."

I laughed. "Go for it, huh? I'm thinking about it. Oh, and about the author's night at the library – you didn't have to do that, but thanks."

"Yes I did." She shrugged and started closing the glass bakery case where she had just removed the donuts. "They weren't recognizing you for your work. It's as simple as that."

"Well, then, it was very kind of you to stand up for me."

"Look, Betsy, you and I are both self-made women. Your husband took a walk, but that never stopped you. I guess I admire that about you. Sometimes you have to make your own happy ending." The bell behind me jingled, and a crowd of ladies dressed in blue scrubs came in.

"You're getting busy, and I completely forgot my second reason for being here." I opened the cookbook, which was now permanently glued by icing to the crocodile page. "I can't get him to stick together. How do I fix it?"

"Um," she said, looking at the picture of the cake, "use icing between each piece to use as a glue, and don't overcook the cakes. If they get all crumbly he'll start to look like he's shedding. Keep it moist, not dry."

"Thanks again, I'll try that." I backed up as the women in blue approached the counter, their eyes focused on their next high-calorie snack. Pattie brushed some flour off of her apron and greeted them. As she started filling their orders she looked over at me and winked. I guess she was making her own happy ending, too.

CHAPTER 4

I stopped over at the Pecan Bayou police station with my box of iced donuts for my dad and George Beckman, the other working officer on our little police force. Dad was tapping away on his computer, while George was putting on his jacket getting ready to go out on patrol. The day dispatcher, Mrs. Thatcher, who still sported a beehive hairdo a la 1963, was filing papers while the squawk of the radio went on behind her. She adjusted her plastic eyeglass frames and focused on the black screen.

"Donuts from PattieCake's!" I announced.

It was like bringing out a cheesecake at the diet center. They all turned toward my pink-striped box, grins lighting up their little law enforcement faces.

"This is mighty nice of you darlin'," my dad said as he picked out a shiny chocolate donut. My dad was the highest-ranking officer on the police force except for the chief of police, Arvin Wilson. Dad handled patrols, court appearances, traffic violations, drugs, domestic disturbances and an occasional murder. The one case he had never solved was the disappearance of my own husband, Barry. He told me he felt he had let me and Zach down. When I discovered the murdered body of my husband's ex-partner last Halloween, I had the opportunity to learn what he was like when he was on a case. He could be grumpy and demanding, but he was smart and sought the truth no matter what.

When I was twelve years old, I decided to try smoking out behind the garage. My dad knew what I had been doing immediately even though I sprayed room freshener everywhere except down my own throat.

"Betsy," he had said. "You haven't been smokin' now, have you?"

"Of course not," I'd answered, wondering if I was blasting him with smoker's breath. I tried to sound wounded that he would ever suspect me of doing such a terrible thing.

"Good to know. By the way, there are some ashes on your shirt."

I brushed off my breast pocket as if there were a swarm of cockroaches on it.

"Gotcha."

My dad reached in for a second donut, barely avoiding George Beckman's big square hand. "You can only take two in the squad car, George," said Mrs. Thatcher. "I don't want to be cleaning up sticky stuff off the equipment again."

George was a large man at over six-foot-three, and he had a cap of blonde hair that was thinning on the top. He wore the Pecan Bayou Police uniform of navy blue, and just the appearance of him in any crowd situation could quiet down some pretty rowdy folks. That is, until he opened his mouth and began speaking. For some reason, George was blessed with a high voice that sometimes made me think of him as a mix between Mickey Mouse and SpongeBob. His lovely voice could be heard in the Episcopal church choir every Sunday morning as he sang in beautiful Irish tenor tones. He squeaked out a resigned "Yes ma'am."

My dad and I walked over to his office. "Can we talk?" I walked in behind him and shut his office door.

"Uh oh, this is never good," he said as he sat in his soft black leather office chair, still balancing the donut between his fingers.

"Fitzpatrick called me yesterday."

"He's done that before, right?"

"Yes, but he has invited me to come to Dallas for the weekend."

"And you've done that before, right?"

"Yes I have, but this time he wants to see me without the boys being around."

He nodded in recognition. "Did you want me to take Zach for the weekend?"

I breathed in deeply and let out a sigh. "I don't know, Dad. I wish I did."

He popped the remainder of the donut in his mouth. "I see. Let me ask you – do you want to go to Dallas?"

"Yes," I answered, blushing. "And no. You know, Dad, this is the first ... time since Barry I've even considered ..."

"I get it, you don't need to go any further with that," he stopped me. "This is something you need to think about, Betsy, but whatever you decide, it's going to be okay."

"I know. Fitzpatrick is a nice guy and all, I'm just not sure I'm ready."

"Would you like to know what I would do if it were me?"

I nodded.

"Go to Dallas. For the last eight years I've watched you work hard, raise my grandson, and even though Barry did what he did, you kept on goin'. I think you deserve to have a little fun in your life. Now mind you, I wouldn't be saying this if I hadn't already done an extensive background check on him."

"Really? You did?"

"You bet your sweet ..." He stopped himself. "Yes I did," he admitted. His face took on a gentle expression I had seen countless times in my life, and it never failed to calm me. He was right – it was time.

That evening, after I put Zach to bed, I picked up the phone and punched in Fitzpatrick's number. I could feel my heart beating through my rib cage and a slight queasiness in my stomach. Why was I acting like this? I was just going to Dallas for a weekend. I certainly had been to Dallas before, right?

The phone rang on the other end. My divorce from Barry had been finalized a year ago, and I was certainly a free woman. My time with Barry had been painful, with his daily criticism of my appearance and just about everything else. I could never be the woman he wanted, and now that I was on this side of it, I wondered why he ever married me. When he disappeared, we all immediately assumed it was some sort of foul play. When I found the box full of bills in the top of his closet, the idea of murder came back to me, but not in the way it had before. It took me years to clean up his financial mess, and I still had to have my dad sign on my house loan in order to get it.

The phone continued to ring. Maybe he wasn't home. It was almost 8:30. Surely he was home.

As I listened to each ring I wondered how many local writers could they really get at the Pecan Bayou Library. Maybe they were paying for writers to come from Houston or Dallas? I thought about my helpful hints book with its quaint blue gingham cover. It was so homey and cute that it might get laughed at next to some artist's rendition of a murder scene or a bodice-ripper cover. If nothing else, this experience would probably prove to be humbling. The phone rang again. That was it – they weren't home, and I was out of my anxiety-producing commitment.

"Hello?" A sultry female voice answered.

"Oh, hi. Um, I might have the wrong number. I'm looking for Leo Fitzpatrick?"

"Yes," she answered, making her Y sound like a J. "He is in the shower right now. He will call you back another time." I heard a click on the other end. I felt a hard lump rising in my throat. Had I been wrong about Fitzpatrick? Was he really just playing me the same way Barry had?

*****

On Friday, after emailing my column to Rocky at the newspaper, I made my final attempt at the crocodile cake. I had to make it work this time. After baking the cake and making sure it was moist enough, I carefully applied some chocolate icing between each connecting layer and gently pushed them together. When I did my final icing, making the cake turn into the green slimy body of a crocodile, I stood back to see if the cracks would form. They did not. I jumped around the kitchen in a little impromptu dance and about fell on the floor when the phone rang.

I looked at the caller ID. It was Fitzpatrick. I was surprised he had enough energy to call after his wild night of abandon with Miss Jes, Jes, Jes. Well, today I was going to be Miss No, No, No. I would tell him where he could stick that weekend in Dallas. I reached for the phone and prepared to push the "on" button, but that feeling of anxiety returned and my stomach knotted up. I felt so nervous my hand froze. I rationalized. He could wait a bit. He could sit and wonder what was going on. Sure, he could wait a bit.

Sometimes I wondered why I even tried. It was certainly safer and a lot less nerve-wracking with just me and Zach. I had people I loved and who loved me. What more could I want? Then I thought about Fitzpatrick and the feeling of his touch on my skin. What else could I want? The phone stopped ringing. Dodged that bullet.

The phone rang again. I couldn't stand it. I jerked it up and punched the talk button. "Who was that woman?" was the first thing that shot out of my mouth, even before the standard greeting of "Hello."

There was a silence on the other end, and then I heard my aunt's voice crackling into the line.

"Betsy? Are you alright?"

I leaned my head against my hand. "Oh, Aunt Maggie. I'm fine. I ... thought you were someone else."

"Obviously. You want to tell me what that was about?"

I pulled out a chair and stared at my green snake-like creation. "Not really, but now that you've happened into the middle of it, I guess I have to."

"Yes, you do."

"I thought you were Fitzpatrick. I called his house Monday night and a woman answered."

"Oh."

"Yes, and when I asked for Leo she told me he was in the shower.

Her voice rose. "Oh."

"And I was going to tell him that I had decided to spend the weekend with him ... without the boys."

Her voice rose again. "Oh! My, my, Betsy."

Then we were both quiet. "You want me to come over?"

I really did, but I knew it wasn't a reasonable request this time of day. "No, you can't leave Danny. I'm okay. "

"No, you're not. I still think there must be an explanation for all of this. There were times when I was hoppin' mad at your Uncle Jeeter only to find out there was a perfectly rational explanation for whatever reason he was driving me crazy."

My Uncle Jeeter had been gone almost four years ago now. He and Aunt Maggie had been married for nearly thirty years when he died. The doctor had told them when they gave birth to Danny, "Having a child with a disability will either make or break you. How's your marriage doing?"

Luckily their marriage was just fine. They also found that dealing with the many issues that came up having a son with Down Syndrome were much easier if they worked together. I looked to their marriage and hoped that my own would be just like it. My marriage was the exact opposite. I wasn't lucky enough to get a Jeeter.

"Just promise me you'll give him a chance to explain," she said.

"Why do I even need an explanation? I mean, it's not like we're married or anything. He's a free agent."

"Stop," my aunt interrupted. "Can you hear yourself? Just because of Barry do you no longer think you have any rights in a relationship?"

"That's not what I meant."

"That's sure how it sounded to me."

"Okay. I'll try to call again, and when I get him I'll ask him who the señorita answering the phone at 8:30 at night is."

"His answer might surprise you."

It sure might, I thought, and it might not be the surprise I was hoping for. I would have believed just about anything, but he was in the shower. If this was the neighbor lady over delivering her latest batch of cookies, the last thing he would do would be to take a shower, right? It wasn't looking good for Mr. Fitzpatrick.

CHAPTER 5

Early on Saturday, I sat behind a folding table in the Pecan Bayou Mall with a banner behind me next to a second empty chair at a matching table to be filled by Vanessa Markham. Her table was identical to mine except for the fact that Vanessa had thought to bring a dark green tablecloth and decorate it with a coordinating grass-skirt garland. I sat behind a naked, melamine-topped, fake walnut table with no tablecloth and no coordinating garland. We were situated in front of some potted palms down the way from some of the other tables on the mall walkway.

I had surrounded my crocodile cake with some bright green recycled plastic grass from Zach's Easter basket to look like the raffia that had showcased the cake in the book. I had added a little blue cellophane wrap to serve as water, making him look like he was in a very shiny swamp. I placed my books on the corner of my table, covering up a nick in the fake walnut.

Vanessa also had a stack of books on the corner of her table. Her chick-lit book was titled *Girl Meets Fifth Avenue*. I was still trying to understand what distinguished "chick literature" from other types. It seemed to be books written for women by women. These books were funny, hip and usually dealt with women's issues like dating, marriage and all those things that make women eat an entire tub of popcorn at chick flicks. Vanessa's book was displayed in kind of a house-of-cards stack on her table. The cover was illustrated with an adorable cartoon portrait of a woman with a shopping bag. I had already seen her sell two books. If she hadn't been so very proud of herself, I would have bought her book myself. The clientele we wrote for were so different from each other. She attracted young twenty-something women who looked like they had just stepped off a display for fine ladies clothing. I garnered grandmothers and young mothers who looked like they were dressed for a long bus trip, with their purses slung across their shoulders and flat shoes, shuffling through the mall.

Vanessa returned to her table with a familiar pink-striped box of cupcakes. "Not for me, of course. My husband loves these things. A girl has to watch her figure." She gestured along her gym-tight body. Today she had on a navy blue form-fitting zip-up sweater with a white blouse underneath and black skinny jeans. On her feet were three-inch heels in black patent leather.

I examined her idea of "creative cooking." Instead of making a cake, she had chosen a Japanese theme with a rock fountain that trickled running water. There were sushi rolls planted around the fountain to resemble the greenery of the peaceful scene. It was so darn tasteful. The only problem was that the constant sound of running water was driving me crazy. I had already been to the bathroom twice. When Vanessa spied my little crocodile cake in the Easter grass she put her hand over her mouth as if it might be a bit of roadkill I had frosted.

"What is that?" she asked, looking at me as if I had an unsightly blemish that had just appeared on my chin.

"Oh," I said, looking down at the cake. "A crocodile."

"Really?" she asked, doubting my credibility. Just as I was about to explain to her what I thought of her sushi fountain, Martha Hoffman walked up to our tables, wearing an oversized sweatshirt that read, "So many books, so little time."

"Vanessa, darling, I just love what you've done showcasing the very essence of Japanese cuisine." Martha beamed. She picked up a copy of *Girl Meets Fifth Avenue* and started paging through it.

"You know I'll have to have a signed copy of your book for the library. The people of Pecan Bayou will be so surprised to know we have such a talented writer in our midst," she aid.

"I'll be glad to sign one for you right now, Martha." Vanessa reached for her rust-colored leather bag behind the table and took out a pen.

"Do you want me to sign it with my real name or my pen name, Vanessa Scarlett?"

"Oh, well, you had better use your pen name. Not everyone knows you personally, as I do." She said it as if she belonged to some elite private club. I had this strange feeling that if Vanessa Markham wasn't trying to get a copy of her book in the library, she wouldn't give Martha Hoffman the time of day. Martha didn't see that, though. The book nerd had finally been accepted at the cheerleader's lunch table. As Vanessa signed her book with a flourish, Martha's eyes drifted to my table and appraised my little crocodile cake. A weak smile my way was all she could muster. She didn't seem to want a copy of my book for her precious stacks.

Vanessa closed the book and handed it to Martha. "Now you just keep your money. My gift to you." Martha held the book tightly and puffed out like a little peacock showing off its plumage. It was all I could take, and besides, the running water was getting to me again.

"I'm heading off to the restroom. Will you watch my table?"

"Again?" Vanessa pouted. "If you must, but don't be gone too long."

I escaped from my post and walked down the mall toward the bathroom. When I came out, I strolled over to Pattie's booth. PattieCake's was in full glory with its pink-striped bunting. Pattie had brought along a high school girl to help her with sales today, and I counted at least twelve trays of cupcakes behind them. They were, by far, the most attended-to table in the mall, with people lining up to purchase Pattie's luscious creations.

Pattie pushed back a strand of hair as she pulled out a loaded tray and plucked out two pink cupcakes with wax paper. As if she could feel my eyes watching her, she glanced my way and upon recognizing me, rolled her eyes and smiled. Even here she was insanely busy. She looked at me as if to say, "Sorry, I'm at it again." Once Pattie filled her orders, she said something to her helper and then came around to the front of the table.

"We decided at the last minute to pack up some cupcakes. Now I'm glad we did. How's traffic at your table?"

"Uh, quiet. Forgot my cupcakes." As if to further humiliate my little green crocodile, on Pattie's table stood an amazing tower of cupcakes. There were six levels, complete with a full-sized layer cake on the top. Each cupcake was frosted with a light yellow frosting, and on their fronts was a delicately sculpted Texas bluebonnet. It was a work of sheer artistry.

"Do you like it? I was up all last night finishing it."

"It's incredible." I answered, feeling as if I had just walked into the Sistine Chapel and decided to look up.

"How did your crocodile cake turn out? Did you get him to stick together?"

"Yes, but he's nothing compared to this. I suppose it doesn't help that I am right next to Vanessa Markham and her sushi fountain."

Pattie shook her head. "Really? A fountain of sushi? How very upscale of her."

"Yeah, well all she really had to do was buy the little fountain, buy the sushi and arrange it all, and yet it is still getting a lot more respect than my little crocodile."

"That's what Vanessa does best. She has an eye for putting things together. That's why she is a fashion writer," Pattie said consolingly.

I thought about the truth of that statement. "That's true."

"It kills me how some of us work so hard to create things and others just buy it and then take credit for it all," Pattie said. She glanced back at her booth and then back to me. "Come on, I want to see your cake and the tribute to rolled-up seaweed." We giggled and walked down the mall arm-in-arm. As we came near the Pecan Bayou Gazette tables, I saw Vanessa speaking to a man with jet-black hair wearing a very dark, very expensive suit. He didn't look like the kind of guy who would read *Girl Meets Fifth Avenue* or the fashion blog, but maybe he was gay or just interested in fashion. He reached out and put his hand around

Vanessa's waist and pulled her close to him. Okay, maybe not gay – and definitely not her husband.

"My, my. Look what we just walked in on," Pattie whispered. A clump of potted palms shielded them from sight for the rest of the mall walkers, but that only worked if you weren't walking up the ramp like we were. As we came closer, Vanessa glanced our way and pulled away from the dark man. He also turned to face us and was even more gorgeous from the front. He had eyes that were nearly black, and when he smiled he revealed white teeth that were accented by the color of his skin.

"Well, I just wanted to tell you how much I loved your book," he said, although no one within ten feet believed him.

"Thank you sir, it's always nice to meet a fan." Vanessa blushed and the stranger walked away.

"Friend of yours?" asked Pattie. "Never saw him before in my life," Vanessa said, as if she were dismissing a waiter.

A neat-looking woman with a pageboy haircut wearing a tan-and-black pantsuit came up to our two tables. This lady was obviously the official Creative Cooks Day judge. She held a clipboard and was busily writing as I scooted behind my table. Pattie waved at me and ran back to her table. The clipboard lady looked down at my little crocodile, who was now losing a gumdrop as the icing melted. She smiled like a polite person looking at an ugly baby.

"How very cute, my dear. I just love his little swamp." She returned to writing on her clipboard, then looked up at the banner behind me and then over to my book. "Oh, I've read your column in the paper. We've used so many of your tips to save money here at the mall. We're all on a budget, you know." She picked up my book from the corner of the table. "We might need a copy of this for the mall office."

Who knew? I had a fan, and it was the judge. Vanessa, who had been watching this entire interchange, cleared her throat loudly. It was probably hard for her to believe my sorry crocodile was getting this much time from the judge.

The judge put down my book and met Vanessa's smile that didn't quite reach her eyes. She turned back to me. "Put one aside for me, Betsy. I'll come back and pay for it later." She said, speaking my first name gingerly as if she had just read it off of the cover of my book.

Vanessa went to the center of her table and started selling the sushi tower. Further down the mall I could see Pattie standing in front of her booth giving me a thumbs-up. "Take that Vanessa!"

"Well, there she is!" Aunt Maggie tapped me on my shoulder. Trailing behind her were Zachary and Danny.

"How did you do, Mom? Did you win?" Zach asked.

Danny walked over to my crocodile cake and spoke gently to it. "Hello Mr. Crocodile. How are you today?"

"Don't get too friendly with it Danny," I said. "Don't forget, he's dessert tonight." Danny chortled. "Okay, Betsy."

Aunt Maggie nudged me. "How did you do?"

"Pretty good I think, but walk down and look at Pattie's. Hers is beautiful."

Both boys craned their necks to see down the mall past the potted palms. "Can we go look at the cupcakes, Mom?" It was only a few feet away, and I could keep an eye on them. "Sure." I said. Danny and Zachary ran down the brown tiled floor to Pattie's cupcake table.

"Boy, that Pattie is always the businesswoman. I see she thought to bring cupcakes to sell. She's a smart one. It's amazing she doesn't have a man by now. She's pretty, successful, and she bakes."

"She's running one of the most successful businesses in Pecan Bayou," I said. "Maybe she doesn't need a man to make her whole."

"You're right. My mother taught me marriage was a career. You were raised differently. It's much better now." Aunt Maggie smiled. "The boys and I walked by the other five displays to check out your competition. There was somebody selling backyard swings who just put out a tray of store-bought cookies. There was Tom Schuller's wife from the Chamber of Commerce who put out a bowl of chili with some crackers, and then her sister-in-law is right next to her representing her husband's car lot with a pot of gumbo and some French bread. Both real nice, but not all that creative. Marcus Daycare has a cute little choo-choo train, but she made it all out of Suzy Qs, so she has about as much work in it as Mrs. Markham's tower of raw fish. All in all Betsy, yours isn't as bad as you may think. For presentation you get a C, but in creativity, you get a B-plus."

I could see the boys had reached the cupcake display and that the judge was heading from Vanessa's table down the walkway to Pattie's.

"Oh, and I forgot. Stanley is here with NUTV. His is pretty creative. His is a green cake with lines on it to look like a football field, and then he put out little plastic players and a tiny TV camera. His cake might give Pattie a run for her money, but only if the judge doesn't notice the grocery store bag in the trash. Stanley bought that cake and put the little football players on it."

I glanced down the mall, and the boys seemed to be counting the cupcakes on Pattie's display. The judge was approaching Pattie as Danny leaned on the table to count the cupcakes on the top-most layer. Just as he put his full weight on the corner of the folding table, I noticed the leg beneath his hand starting to buckle. Within seconds the entire stack of cupcakes came down on top of Danny and Zachary, leaving them buried in a mishmash pile of cake and icing.

Maggie and I raced down to Danny and Zach, who were struggling to get up from the mess on the floor. Zach slipped in the yellow-and-blue icing, further smearing it into the tiles. He tried to stand up again, balancing on wobbly legs.

"What happened?" I asked. The entire crowd around Pattie's booth had shifted their focus to the icing-covered Danny and Zach. The judge was clucking her tongue and shaking her head as she put a big X over Pattie's page.

"I'm so sorry," said the judge. "I needed to at least have had a look at your creation. I'll have to take you out of the competition."

Pattie's face grew flushed as her mouth gaped open. She had by far the best entry in the contest, and now my family was responsible for destroying it.

"Oh, Pattie. We're sorry," Aunt Maggie said. Zach and Danny were both near tears. Danny took Pattie's hand in his icing-covered grasp. "Miss PattieCake. We are real sorry. We didn't mean to hurt your cupcakes. I just put my hand on the table, that's all."

I looked back at the upturned table. Three of the legs were locked into position, but one was slid back, leaving it unlocked.

"Look at these table legs," I said, kneeling down. "All of the others are perfectly straight except for this one here. It seems this table leg wasn't locked into place. The first person to lean on the table would tip it over. Now maybe it just wasn't set up right, but if that was so, the cupcake tower would have collapsed when Pattie placed it on the table. Could it be that someone purposely slid the lock off, causing the table to collapse when any weight was put on it?"

"Tsk, tsk," Vanessa had joined us. "You really should be more careful about locking those table legs into place, Pattie. What a terrible shame." She pursed her lips together. "What a shame." It struck me as just a bit rehearsed.

"I guess that just leaves the rest of us in the competition. Betsy, you really should watch your child," Vanessa added.

"Just what are you saying?" I asked.

"These things do happen my dear, especially when children go unsupervised."

There was a menacing quiet between the two of us that seemed to spread throughout the mall. The longer the silence lasted, the more I felt we were about to have a slap down. Had Vanessa jimmied with the leg of Pattie's table, making it an accident waiting to happen? If she did, what a perfect foil having my son and cousin at the table. Vanessa had seemed a little sneaky, but I couldn't believe she would do all that just to win a stupid mall contest.

"You were over here earlier, Vanessa. Who's to say you didn't mess with the leg so that the first person who leaned on the table would capsize Pattie's cupcakes?"

"Are you accusing me of sabotage? That would be pretty convenient for you, considering you and your family purposely took the best exhibit out of the competition."

That was it – I was taking her down. I walked toward her.

"Nevertheless," the judge broke the impending feeling of confrontation in the air. "I'm sure all these lovely people still want to buy up all of your cupcakes, Pattie. She turned to the people in line. "Everybody, can we have a round of applause for PattieCake's?" The crowd broke out into applause and a few cheers. Pattie turned to them and smiled, taking a little bow.

"Tell you what," said Aunt Maggie. "I'll take the boys to go get washed up, and why don't you help your friend Pattie clean up?" I nodded and started loading the collapsed pieces of the cupcake tower into a big green rubber trashcan the mall custodian had pulled up for us.

Vanessa came over to me. "I'll head back to our tables. I'm sure I must have some book customers by now."

"I'm sure." I said.

The mall judge moved down the walkway to the next exhibitor. Pattie heaved a sigh and rolled her eyes. "I can't believe it. I've been punked."

"Yes, you were, and I think we both know who did it."

"That woman is evil," Pattie said, watching Vanessa slink down the mall in her clickety-clack heels.

"She's so competitive. Evilly competitive, but competitive."

"She's in my shop at least twice a week buying those German Chocolate cupcakes. That's it. She's cut off."

We both laughed.

It was only a few minutes later when the judge came over the mall's loudspeaker. The winner of the Creative Cooks contest was Vanessa Markham and her little Zen fountain of raw fish. She had to win at any cost, even if that cost was my friend Pattie.

CHAPTER 6

On Tuesday, after our slippery fun at the mall over the weekend, I was working to put a few notes on index cards for my upcoming "Author Night at the Library." I didn't want to get up there and start babbling. Maybe I wasn't a "real" author, but I could certainly talk about my subject area. I had gathered some statistics about helpful hints and how many people use books like mine to get through their daily routines.

I had also come up with some tips for the library, not because I felt like being particularly helpful, but because I wanted to irritate Martha Hoffman. Hmmm, their use of light was not very energy-efficient. I recalled looking for a book on the second floor of the library, where the temperature seemed to be several degrees hotter than the downstairs. Part of that had to do with the big picture windows, which we all loved. Nevertheless, a little tinting might be just the answer to lower the temperature – and the electric bills.

I heard Zach walk into the kitchen behind me. I waited for him to speak, but for once he was silent. When I turned toward him, he had to have had every straw we owned bulging out of his mouth and cheeks. How many did I buy in a pack? A hundred? Five hundred?

"Zach, what are you doing?" He tried to answer me, but that caused a few straws to fall haphazardly out.

Danny walked in holding an empty plastic bag that had a big "100 Straws" logo printed on the outside. Had they gone out and bought a new bag, or had Danny brought them from his house?

"We need you to look up on your computer, Betsy," Danny said.

"What am I looking up?"

"We need you to look up the straw record."

I sighed and walked to the next room, where my home office was. I had redecorated what would have been a formal dining room back in the fifties. Now it was an informal office for me with light green walls, a white desk that held my laptop and printer, and in the middle of the wall I had the only picture I owned of my grandmother before she died. It was silly, but somehow I felt we connected in some distant way each time I sat down to work. I searched "world record for drinking straws in mouth."

"Okay, guys, according to the Guinness Book of World Records, some guy in Munich, Germany holds the record."

"How many?" asked Danny.

"Four hundred," I answered. "How many are in Zach's mouth?" Zach held up seven fingers and then five. "Seventy-five?"

His lips looked stretched as it was. I started worrying if his face really would stick that way.

"I don't know, bud. I think your child-sized mouth may just be a little too small for this challenge. This guy in the picture looks like he has a wider-than-average adult mouth." With that, Zach spit out all of the remaining seventy-five straws onto the floor. On to the next record, I thought.

"Aw, Mom. We're never going to break a record." He balled his hands into fists.

"As long as it doesn't cause injury to you, like permanently stretching out your lips, I'd say keep trying," I told him. "I know – you could be the kid with the cleanest room for the longest period of time!"

Zach rolled his eyes at me and threw himself down on the small green couch that leaned against the wall. "Don't turn this into another chore thing!" He didn't appreciate my humor. Danny followed suit and threw himself on the remaining cushions.

"Keep thinking, guys. You'll come up with something."

My phone rang at my elbow. "Miss Livingston? This is Martha Hoffman at the library. I got your number from Pattie. I just wanted to let you know, we have quite a few speakers tonight, and because you are such a late entry, we'll have to put you at the end of the program.

Now, we want the program to end at 10 p.m., so there is a possibility we might run out of time before we get to you. We felt it was important to put the, um, more established writers first. You do understand, don't you?"

I sure did. "I understand completely."

Pattie had them over a barrel by making her appearance based on mine. It probably didn't help my status that I argued with her beloved Vanessa over the weekend. My book probably did people a lot more good on a daily basis than all of the others combined, leaving out Pattie's cookbook, of course.

"Well, good then. I guess we'll be seeing you this evening in the main lecture room of the library. We expect quite a turnout. You do know where we're located?"

"Yes, I do," I answered. In a little town like this, how could this woman and I not have come in contact before? Did she think I had never been to the library? I would be sure to wear my overalls and black out one of my teeth just so I could meet her expectations of me.

*****

After leaving Zach with my father for the evening, I drove to the library just as the sun was setting over the downtown area. Shopkeepers were turning the closed signs in their windows, while restaurants like Benny's Barbecue were entertaining friends, old and new. Maybe I should have told Martha Hoffman I was too busy to make this thing and spare myself the ridicule, but after we had just destroyed Pattie's cupcake tower, I was a little duty-bound myself. Pattie had stuck up for me, and now I could at least do her the courtesy of being there.

Our town library was really quite nice, considering the size of Pecan Bayou. We had two floors, the upper floor containing nonfiction and biographies and the bottom floor fiction and a lovely children's section with sliding accordion doors to shut out the noise of any of the children's programs. I noticed some new bookshelves as I walked by. It was about time they redecorated the children's part of the library. Zach loved going to pick out books here, although I couldn't ever remember checking out books with Martha Hoffman. It was hard to imagine her doing "Story Hour" with the kids.

I walked to the back of the fiction section where the meeting room was situated. Normally there was a large table in the middle of this room, but for the crowd expected, they had moved it out and replaced it with folding chairs. The room had the comfortable smell of old books. All of the walls were lined with the antique book archive in sedate colors of maroon, black and forest green. The gilt lettering was simple yet elegant. It would be a pleasant place to sit and read away the hours with the soft but efficient lighting and muffled quiet of the room. I took in a deep breath, feeling at peace, then I looked up front and noticed all the chairs at the presenters' table seemed to be filled except one. I also noticed Vanessa Markham was not up there yet. If I didn't hurry, that would mean there wouldn't be a chair up there for me. My moment of peace shattered.

The audience chairs were stacked six across with a little aisle down the middle. As I walked down the aisle, Ruby Green reached out and took my hand. "Hi Betsy. We have room in our row if you're lookin' for a seat." Ruby had probably come straight from The Best Little Hair House in Texas. Her auburn hair was teased up an inch and a half around her head, and tonight she wore her red-framed glasses and a black zebra silk scarf.

"Thank you. That's so nice of you, but I'm supposed to be up front." Right as I said that, Vanessa came running up the aisle past me and headed for the speaker's table.

"Oh, are you an author?" Ruby asked me.Vanessa laughed as she ran by us. "Don't let her kid you, Ruby. She doesn't write real fiction. Unless she's telling stories about magically collapsing tables full of cupcakes."

She clicked up the aisle effortlessly, like a butterfly gliding to a flower. I trudged behind her, speaking to her back. "I wasn't making anything up, Vanessa. We all knew who messed with that table." My voice level rose as I followed on her heels to the front, directing the crowd's attention toward us.

Martha Hoffman shushed me violently, probably using half of her mouth's capacity for spit. She had been sorting through a stack of handouts for the audience. Vanessa quickly slid into the one vacant chair, leaving me standing there. She smoothed her skirt, sat with perfect posture and tossed back her lustrous hair. I stood there awkwardly. "Miss Hoffman, where did you want me to sit?" I asked.

The librarian looked up from her handouts, smile glued to her face. Her voice was as sweet as what comes in the pink packets with your coffee. "Oh, dear. I forgot about you, Becky." She glanced at the long table filled by the other authors. "I suppose we could add you over there on the end."

I looked to the end of the table, where Pattie was sitting next to a dark man in black turtleneck. Not a very comfortable shirt for South Texas, but somehow on this guy it worked. He seemed so familiar to me. Where had I seen him before? Pattie raised her elbow and waved trying not to jab the dark man in the ribs.

Martha took a chair off the front row of the audience and wedged it into the corner by Pattie.

"Really, Miss Hoffman. I don't mind sitting out in the audience."

"Don't be ridiculous, dear. You're an ... a presenter, just like the rest of my guests tonight."She flung her arm toward the chair, which was supposed to be a gesture of kindness but felt more like an order to sit down – *now*. I squeezed in next to Pattie, pulling my own elbows in and holding my purse on my lap.

"She forgot," Pattie whispered, not sounding as if she totally believed it. "What a surprise," I whispered back.

A brown hand extended to me across Pattie's front.

"Good evening." The dark man's Hispanic accent was rich and flowing. He leaned forward to meet my eyes. "I am Damien Perez, the author of the *Camazotz Chronicles*."

I had no idea what a Camazotz was and why it needed to be chronicled. It must have shown in my face, because he continued.

"Mexican vampire fiction, my dear." His voice was also familiar. Down the table, Vanessa Markham's glance turned toward the two of us. This was the man she had been embracing in the mall. It had to kill her that he was sitting so close to me and Pattie.

"Oh," I said placing my hand in his. "Betsy Livingston, Helpful Hints."

"Nice to meet you, Betsy Livingston." He dripped charm, reminding me of Bela Lugosi inviting the stranded travelers in for a bite. Pattie cleared her throat, and we quickly dropped hands.

Martha Hoffman stood in front of the table and addressed the curious – or maybe somewhat bored – citizens of Pecan Bayou. My Aunt Maggie had come in and was now sitting in the seat Ruby Green had offered to me. When I caught her eye, she waved excitedly as if I had just hit the big time in authordom. I waved back slowly, so as not to further draw the attention of the entire crowd now staring directly at us.

"Welcome, ladies and gentlemen." Martha Hoffman put her hands together under her chin to show her sheer delight at the attendance of author night. Her cheeks pudged out at each side, making her look like a happy chipmunk. "Tonight, at our first annual author's night, we will be hearing from all kinds of writers."

Martha turned to face the other end of the table, where a scrawny-looking man with bug eyes held tightly to a stack of papers.

"We have Mr. Oscar Larry, our resident UFO aficionado, who has penned the book *I Saw It With My Own Eyes*, in which he recounts his experience with an extraterrestrial." The audience clapped in respect.

"We also have Destiny Wood, also known as Edith Martin from Andersonville. She writes some pretty steamy romance novels. Dashing men and beautiful women living adventurous lives are all over her pages." Edith Martin pulled at her closely cropped gray hair. She was thin, bony and in her fifties, and she reminded me of my fourth-grade teacher. She raised her shoulders in a giggle as Martha described her. This is why we see so few author pictures on the backs of romance novels. Just goes to show you don't have to look like a movie star to write romance.

"Next to Destiny Wood we have our own Vanessa Markham. She is our best girlfriend in predicting the latest styles and fads, and if that weren't enough, Vanessa also writes under the pen name of Vanessa Scarlett. Vanessa has written what I think will be the breakout 'chick-lit' novel of the year, *Girl Meets Fifth Avenue*. I couldn't put it down, Vanessa. It was simply the best book I have read in a long time!" They exchanged glances as if they had a secret no one else knew. As much as Martha seemed to slough me off as a bug on her windshield, she seemed to idolize Vanessa.

"If you are a fan of vampire fiction," Martha said, " then we have Mr. Damien Perez, author of the *Camazotz Chronicles*, a gripping set of books about Mexican vampires." Ruby Green sat up in her folding chair and flashed what I would have to call an attempt at a seductive smile at Damien Perez, the man in the black turtleneck.

"Next to Señor Perez, ladies and gentlemen, we have our very favorite diet buster Pattie Jackson, the owner of PattieCake's Bakery. She will be discussing her cookbook and how she makes all of those delicious baked goods. She also brought us some samples of her exquisite work for you to enjoy tonight." The crowd oohed and clapped.

Martha's gaze shifted to me. "If all of that wasn't enough, we also have blog writer Becky Livingston to talk to us about helpful hints in the home." She turned back to the gathered group. "Let's have a big hand for all of our authors!"

The crowd clapped as Pattie whispered into my ear, "Doesn't that old cow know your name, yet, Betsy?"

"Guess not," I whispered back, smiling at my aunt, who was trying to get the crowd into a standing ovation. Nothing like having relatives in the audience.

CHAPTER 7

Oscar Larry, who sat at the other end of the table, was the first presenter of the evening. I knew we were in trouble when he started setting up a laptop and projector to show some of his research. He also passed out little coasters with the name of his store in San Antonio, "Sky Lights – the ultimate resource for your extraterrestrial needs."

"Even though we think of UFOs as something from second-rate creature features on the midnight movies, they are real, mysterious objects that have been observed in our skies since the earliest days of our recorded history," he intoned. "Tonight I am so pleased to get to share with you all of my scientific observations and extensive resources on the subject."

Did that mean what I thought it meant? Did Martha tell any of the other authors there would be a time limit on their presentations? I guess she never actually gave me a limit, just a suggestion there would be no time for me. This could be a long night. I grabbed my cell phone out of my purse and started texting my dad. If I was going to run late, I needed to let him know. Judging by the median age of our audience, running late may not work too well with them, either. We definitely had some eight o'clock bedtime folks here.

My phone lit up with an incoming text. I had turned off the sound so no one listening to Oscar Larry's droning on would realize I was involved in a conversation elsewhere. I expected it to be a text from my father griping at me for extending his babysitting time, but instead it was from Leo Fitzpatrick in Dallas:

> *Betsy. Tried to call you, but you weren't home. Have you come to a decision?*

Oh boy. I did have some thoughts on the matter, but I didn't know if you could get in trouble with the phone company for texting four-letter words. This was it. I could ask him about the woman who answered the phone, but if I did, what would he think of me? It wasn't like we were living in the same town or anything, and it wasn't like we were serious enough to warrant not seeing other people. But still, I felt cheated on somehow.

I had not been involved with a man in quite a while, and I needed to feel safe in my first jump into the dating pool. I had already lived with a guy who had betrayed my trust, and even though I felt I was past all that, I still had these little nagging doubts in the back of my head that I really wasn't good enough. Look at tonight – I was the add-on author. I wasn't the beloved fashion blogger. I was that woman who could tell you how to unclog your sink – that is, once she got her own sink unclogged. Not so glamorous. No wonder Fitzpatrick was seeing another woman in Dallas.

The words on the cell phone seemed to be shouting at me, "Have you come to your decision? Have you? Have you?" Oscar Larry was turning out the lights to show exciting footage of his own personal UFO sighting. How thrilling, except now the room would notice my phone was lit up on my lap. I quickly punched "end" and stuffed the phone back in my purse.

I settled down for the next 30 minutes to view what looked like blurry pie tins floating through the atmosphere. That's it! Betty Crocker was an alien. Now we had the delicious proof of it. Who's next? Mrs. Fields? Marie Callender? The Gorton's fisherman? Would the controversy ever end?

When the lights came back on, I reached back into my purse for my phone. Oscar Larry was now passing out thick stacks of photocopies to his captive audience. Half of Ruby's crowd from the Hair House were groggily passing along Larry's handouts. Where was Martha Hoffman during this, and why wasn't she cutting this guy off? Doing a search of the room, both she and Vanessa Markham were absent from the world's longest book talk. They were probably out dusting off that copy of the best novel Martha had ever read.

Oscar Larry started in again. "They might have closed Project Blue Book in 1969 because of what they called a lack of evidence, but I think ..." And on and on and on he went, discussing each and every sighting in American history. I went back to my phone. I had received two messages in the time the lights were out. The first was from Fitzpatrick, repeating what he'd said in the first text. He really wanted to know. I pictured him leaning over his phone reading my texts with those beautiful blue eyes, pushing his light brown hair from his forehead. I felt myself drifting into Destiny Wood's territory. Then I pictured a dark-haired beauty answering his phone telling me he was in the shower. I decided to ignore him for just a little bit longer.

I heard a loud yawn from the audience as Oscar Larry continued. Martha Hoffman came back into the room, followed by Vanessa, who quietly took her chair. Martha didn't look as smitten with Vanessa as she had been earlier in the evening. I wondered if Vanessa finally told her she only liked her for her library. Martha looked at her watch, and her face took on a pained expression.

I checked my second text, this one from my father:

Zach and Danny tried to break the world record for eating boiled eggs. Where is the antacid?

Martha Hoffman was striding toward the speakers' table from the back of the room. "And thank you so much, Mr. Larry for your ... detailed description of the world of aliens."

"But I wasn't finished yet," Oscar Larry stuttered, his face reddening as he realized he would leave us uninformed about space aliens. He still hadn't told us the five-note sequence to play on our kazoos when the giant crafts landed.

"No, no, Mr. Larry. We need to save something for the people who will read your book now, mustn't we?" Larry looked disappointed, but then the realization came over him that people would have to buy his book to read it. He nodded vigorously and sat back down.

"Oh, dear where does the time go? It seems we are going to have reschedule our author night for next week so that we can hear from the rest of our panelists," said Martha." She turned toward the rest of us at the table. "Authors, can we count on you to come back next week to speak about your life's work?" Everyone looked to each other and nodded in agreement. Great, another night of literary abandon. I didn't know if I could take it.

"Then it's all settled. We will all meet back here next week to visit with the rest of our esteemed guests and try to budget our time a little more appropriately." The remaining audience clapped. I noticed several chairs were now empty, probably finding the slide show a good time to slip out unnoticed, just as our hostess had.

As soon as we were dismissed, I rose from my chair and told Aunt Maggie of the twin bellyaches we were about to encounter. "Will those two ever stop?" Maggie sighed.

"They might end up being the most notable record-breakers in the emergency room," I answered.

*****

When Maggie and I got to the house, we found both boys lying on the couch holding their midsections. "Oooh, this was a bad idea," said Zach.

"Where did you get enough eggs to break a record?"

"We didn't have enough, we just wanted to see if we could eat enough to get close to the record."

"How many is the record?"

"Sixty-five in seven minutes."

"How many did you eat?" Danny held up five fingers. "You each ate five eggs?" Maggie asked.

"I ate five, Zach ate four," said Danny. "Oooh," repeated Zach.

My dad, the Texas gun-totin' all-around tough guy, started giggling.

"They asked me to boil 'em all the eggs in the refrigerator. I didn't expect them to eat 'em all at once. You two characters shoulda thought this one out." My dad spooned up some pink antacid medicine for each of the potential record-breakers to swallow.

"I think this is all silly," said Aunt Maggie. "The sooner you boys stop trying to break some fool record, the sooner you'll be safer from yourselves."

"Mama, we'll be famous," said Danny.

"There's a lot more important things in this world than being famous."

"Yeah, like being rich," Zach added.

My father started laughing again. "Good to know you've raised these boys right."

"Don't encourage them, Judd." Maggie said.

"Sorry, but you have to admit it is pretty funny. How was your author talk, Betsy?"

"I wouldn't know. I never had a chance to talk."

Aunt Maggie sat down on the couch next to Danny and started patting his hand. "Some looney UFO fella got up there first and bored us all to death with his out-of-focus pictures."

"Why Maggie, I'm surprised at you, who purports to believe in the paranormal," said my dad.

"This is totally different, Judd, and you know it," Maggie replied. "This guy was loco, and the worst part was he took the entire evening. Our little Betsy didn't get to utter one word. She would have been the best one up there."

"I'm pretty sure there were four other very good authors waiting to speak before me," I said, "but don't worry, the librarian made us all promise to come back again next week."

"So I'm the lead babysitter next week, too?"

"If you don't mind, Daddy. Pattie said she wouldn't talk about her book unless I got to do the same. She brings the cupcakes for the evening, which makes me a necessary inconvenience for Martha Hoffman."

My dad's cell phone went off, and I could tell from the expression on his face it was the police department. He answered and went into the next room. My aunt helped Danny come off the couch. "We'd better get home too, Betsy."

"Did you notice the librarian and Vanessa Markham went out during the presentation?"

"No. Maybe if she had stayed she would have shut loony Larry up."

My dad returned to the living room. "Looks like you got home just in time. I need to head out."

"Is everything okay?" I asked. Being the daughter of a policeman, I had my share of anxiety when he took a call like this at night. Even in small towns, bad things could happen.

"Sure, darlin'. It's just something on an old case that George needs some help on, that's all." He reached over and gave me a quick hug and then bent down to Zach on the couch and tweaked his nose. "Stay out of the eggs, partner. I think you've had enough cholesterol to last you 'til you're twelve."

CHAPTER 8

The next day I had to go by the newspaper office to pick up my paycheck from Rocky Whitson. The Pecan Bayou Gazette office was a two-story brick building located at the end of Main Street. The paper had served our community proudly since 1955. The bottom floor of the office served as the "newsroom" with a mottled assortment of mismatched desks, each with a computer. Stacks of paper, newspapers and reference books were everywhere. The top floor served as an archive, storing papers that dated back for fifty years.

Rocky's desk was in the very back of the newsroom, facing the other four desks. Peter Markham, who sat across from Rocky, covered all the sports in town, from Little League to the high school championship of every sport. There was also a high school girl who came in one afternoon a week to work on the classified advertising. Rocky handled the circulation and did general reporting. He'd hired a kid from the junior college to set up the website, which he then maintained himself. He could update daily on the web in addition to the standard weekly issue. It was a winning situation for the paper, but it was still a lot of hard work for Rocky, and unless he won the lottery, he would never be rich.

Rocky wore a plaid shirt in muted browns and golds with a white T-shirt underneath. He reminded me of old photos of my father from the '60s. Rocky would have looked more suited to a plow than a newsroom, but he was a reporter who had dutifully recorded history in these parts. The day JFK was shot in Dallas, Rocky was there covering the story for the paper. His pictures of Kennedy and his wife were now a part of the national collection at the Smithsonian. When the boy did the shooting from the University of Texas clock tower, Rocky knew some of the students who were there that day. Their first-hand accounts appeared in the Gazette, and the stories were picked up by papers all over the world. He was a legend in this town, yet he looked like a farmer.

As I walked in, Rocky was busy working at his desk. When he saw me he quickly reached into a drawer and pulled out an envelope. Peter Markham was watching videos of football on his computer and dully nodded as I walked by.

"Needin' that cold, hard cash there, Betsy?" Rocky handed me the envelope and leaned back in his squeaky black leather chair. "Now try not to spend it all in one place," he joked.

"That's getting harder and harder."

"Loved the column you wrote about getting rid of moths. Old Simmons down at the hardware store loved it even more. He said he's sold out of cheesecloth and all the stuff that goes in it. He told me he'd like to know what you're going to write about next so he can stock up."

"Glad I could be of help," I said.

Vanessa Markham stomped into the office, slamming the door. Today she had on a tangerine-and-white print dress with a short white jacket flapping as she strode over to Peter and slapped a piece of paper down on his desk. He rolled back in his office chair.

"What the hell is this?" she demanded.

There is just nothing like being trapped in a room when a married couple decides to have it out, I thought.

"A receipt?" he answered dumbly.

"That's right, a receipt from the Worthington Arms in San Marcos."

San Marcos is where all the best shopping outlets were in this part of Texas. Had Peter been on a little shopping spree and then decided to spend the night? In my own marriage, some of the most bitter fights were about money.

"Right, sweetie. Remember I was there covering the state football championship."

"You were there covering the championship in December. This receipt is for February," she said.

"Uh ..." A line of sweat appeared above his lip. "Right. Well, let me check my calendar to see what I was doing there that weekend." He rolled up to his desk and pulled up his calendar on his screen.

Vanessa rolled him back around to face her. "Don't bother. You told me you were in Corpus Christi that weekend visiting your cousin Charlie. Funny, I didn't know you and ol' Chuck had a yen for outlet shopping."

"No, no, I think you're mistaken."

"I'm not mistaken about anything and you know it."

I heard Rocky clear his throat behind me in an attempt to make Vanessa aware that we were both observing this scene. Vanessa glanced up, finally registering that I was in the office standing next to Rocky. She straightened the lapels of her white jacket as if she were challenging me to say something.

"Peter, why don't you take an early lunch with your Missus?" Rocky suggested.

Peter's head jerked back. "Yeah. Sure, boss." He grabbed his jacket off the back of his chair while Vanessa stormed out the door ahead of him. After all of the feelings of insecurity she caused in me, I couldn't imagine what it would be like to be married to her. Peter was a handsome, athletic man. He was just the kind of person who would attract Vanessa in her way of acquiring all that makes a person look good. That would also mean that Peter would attract other women, and if he wasn't feeling good about his marriage, it was just possible he was cheating on her.

"Glad you're single, Betsy. This old man couldn't take watching another scene like that this morning."

"I'm pretty glad about it myself," I said. "Have they ever fought like that before?"

"Some, but I have to say that was the biggest one yet." He scratched the side of his head.

"Hell hath no fury like Vanessa scorned."

"Guess you know that first-hand," Rocky chuckled.

*****

My second evening preparing for author night at the library, I wasn't half as nervous as the first. I had my index cards prepared and some business cards with my blog address on it. I had a list of the three bookstores in the area where my book was available. Okay, one of the stores also sold bait, but that was just an added incentive, right? The sweet smell of success. It also didn't hurt that I had seen Vanessa in a major brawl with her husband. Everyone had their little troubles, even Vanessa Scarlett, Chick Lit Sweetheart.

My screen door creaked. "Ready for another night of little green men there, Betsy?" my dad said as he and Aunt Maggie came in with Danny, who was holding a mesh laundry bag stuffed with what looked to be socks of all colors.

"We're going to break a record, Betsy," my cousin said, a look of great importance on his sweet face.

"What record are you trying for tonight, Danny? Matching socks for the land-speed record?"

Zach came into the kitchen from the den. "No," he said, sarcasm in his voice as if any idiot knows that matching socks is actually a chore and no kid in his right mind would do that on purpose. "Mom, we are going to break the record for how many socks can be put on a single foot. According to the book, some woman in Ireland holds the record at 126. Piece of cake."

"That coming from the guy who dove head-first into cake at the mall."

"We told you that wasn't our fault," said Zach.

"Not our fault," echoed Danny.

"I know, I know," I said, thinking about whose fault it really was.

My home phone rang on the counter. Danny ran to it and answered, "Livingstons. How can I help you?"He listened for a minute and then said, "Okay, I'll get her for you, Mr. Fitzpatrick."He handed the phone to me. "It's Tyler's dad." "Thanks," I said, pressing my lips into a thin line and slowly taking the phone.

"Come on boys, let's go count those socks," Maggie said, rounding up the boys and heading toward the den. My dad didn't move until Maggie came back and yanked into the next room.

"I finally got you on the phone," Fitzpatrick said.

"Sorry I haven't gotten back to you," I said. "Crazy week. I'm about to head out the door now."

"Really? I was hoping we would have a chance to talk about you coming up for the weekend. Look, I sense you backing off in this and well, if you're not comfortable with it, I just want you to know that's okay."

That was so sweet and just like the Leo Fitzpatrick I got to know last fall. It was so hard for me to believe he had more than one relationship going at the same time, but there so many things about Barry I never would have believed when I was married to him.

"That's very nice of you to say. I want you to know I have been thinking about it, and I need to ask you a question."

"Go ahead. Ask me anything." That seemed honest enough.

"I just wanted to know if ... you might ... have a girlfriend in Dallas." There. It was out, even if it did sound like teen anxiety asking if he had a "girlfriend."

The other end of the line was quiet. Then Fitzpatrick spoke. "Fair enough question," he conceded. "At present, I don't have a girlfriend, although there is a really nice single mom I took a shine to a few months ago."

"There is?"

"It's you." He laughed, and finally, so did I."Listen, Betsy. I work a lot covering this crazy Texas weather. The other night I got called out at 7:30 to go cover a tornado sweeping through the area. I don't have time for too many women in my life."

"A tornado?"

"You know, a rotating column of air ranging in width from a few yards to more than a mile and whirling at destructively high speeds, usually accompanied by a funnel-shaped downward extension of a cumulonimbus cloud."

If I hadn't known, I did now. "What night was that?"

"Last Tuesday, I think. I had to call in Mrs. Alvarez to watch Tyler."

"Mrs. Alvarez?"

"Yes, she's a sweet lady in our neighborhood that all the kids call 'Grandma.' Taylor really felt comfortable with her, so I asked her if she would get him off the bus after school and cook dinner for us every day. She's a godsend."

"I'll say," I murmured, agreeing on more than one level.

"So what about our weekend?"

"I think ... it sounds like a wonderful idea. Plan on it."

CHAPTER 9

This week as I entered the library, I had Aunt Maggie along with me. We walked past the accordion-fold door that closed off the children's section and into the library's meeting room. We had a smaller audience tonight but had gained Peter Markham. Pattie was already up front and was gesturing to an empty chair saved just for me.

Martha Hoffman was looking at her wristwatch and glancing around the room. There were still two empty seats waiting for Vanessa Markham and Edith Martin, the romance writer. Oscar Larry sat in his chair typing furiously into a laptop with an alien sticker glaring at us on the raised lid. Damien Perez sat quietly, examining his fingernails on one hand. With a wary glance from Martha Hoffman, I scurried to my seat next to Pattie.

"I'll bet you're the one she wanted to be late," Pattie whispered into my ear.

"At least my presentation takes ten minutes and not three hours," I whispered.

"Thank God for that," Damien Perez whispered to both of us in his low voice. The three of us laughed, making Martha Hoffman turn around and give us the official librarian "shhhhh."

Edith Martin came scurrying into the room wearing a red woven scarf, a turquoise blouse and a full printed skirt over boots. She glanced out at the audience and then slid into her seat. She put her hand over her heart as she caught her breath. Martha Hoffman looked out into the main library one more time and then turned back to the crowd.

"Well, it seems Vanessa Scarlett must be running a little late, so we will go ahead and begin," the librarian said. "Last week we had a detailed discussion about UFOs from Mr. Oscar Larry." He stood up to comment, but Martha gestured for him to take his seat. "Tonight we will hear many more speakers, starting with Destiny Wood, known locally as Edith Martin. She will be discussing her steamy romance novels." Martha Hoffman's voice rose at the end to emphasize the guilty-pleasure aspect of Edith's writing. Miss Ruby and her crowd, who had come back for an encore performance, rustled around in the metal folding chairs. Edith stood and walked to the center of the room.

"I have written historical romance novels for the last ten years. You may have read some of my books, *Victory with the Viscount, Duke of Love* or *Mistress of the Manor.* Tonight, I wanted to read a scene from the novel I am writing presently, *London's Man of Trouble."*

She opened a file folder and began to read: "I ran into his strong arms, his muscles bulging as he brought his large hands over my body. I felt a warmth spread through me as I surrendered to his embrace ..."

Edith went on and on, describing the act of lovemaking in such detail that I noticed many of the members of the audience looking a little hot around the collar. One person I didn't expect a reaction from was Peter Markham. He seemed to be glued to her every word and bit his lip as she described the very throes of passion. Edith was now in full dramatic portrayal of the scene with the back of her hand placed upon her forehead: "Georgina said, yes, yes, yes!"

"Yes!" Martha Hoffman shouted. "I mean," in a softer voice, "yes, I think that gives us quite a taste of your ... sensual style of writing. Thank you so much. Why don't we all take ten minutes. Maybe some of us need a smoke break after all that ... uh, ten minutes, everyone."

Pattie stood up. "I brought some of my orange dream cupcakes and left them upstairs on the big study table for everybody." The crowd rose happily to go upstairs for cupcakes. I checked my phone to see that a picture had been texted over to me. Zach looked like he had elephantiasis trying to pull another sock on his foot. "That kid," I said. I walked over to Aunt Maggie and tilted the phone so that she could see the picture.

"Oh my. I don't think they thought about how stretched out a sock would have to be to go over twenty other socks."

"Aunt Maggie, they are driving me crazy with this stuff. I wish there was a record they could break without killing themselves."

"I know, me too."

"Maggie?" Ruby Green stuck her head in the door. "Come upstairs and get a cupcake before they're all gone. I want you to meet my new beau, Mr. Florence."

"Be right there." Maggie touched me on the arm. "Why don't you go over to the children's section and find one those record books. Maybe you can find something tame for them to do."

Not needing the cupcakes, I agreed. "Good idea."

As I started walking out of the meeting room, Martha Hoffman stopped me. "Are you the reason Vanessa didn't get here for my author's night?"

"Excuse me?" Why would I have anything to do with Vanessa Markham getting to a meeting?

"Well, I just asked her husband, Peter, and he said something about the two of you having a fight in the mall."

"Did he? Well that fight was weeks ago and really wasn't that much of a big deal. I'm surprised Vanessa didn't share that with you. Pattie's cupcake tower collapsed because your BFF Vanessa was the one who messed with the table leg and set her up so she could win with that sorry fish fountain of hers."

Martha gasped, and the remaining stragglers hurried to get out of the room and avoid getting caught in our argument.

"How dare you!"

"Listen, Martha, I don't know why Vanessa isn't here. Why don't you try calling her? I'm sure she must be on your speed dial." I pushed past her, taking a deep breath. I knew this lady didn't like me, but blaming me for Vanessa's no-show seemed a little out there. Why would Peter point to me as the reason his wife was tardy? Didn't he know where she was? That was a truly strange marriage, especially with him visiting hotels in San Marcos and her hanging out with the vampire hunter. I thought I had had a bad marriage. They were both such physically attractive people, but inside all that beauty was another matter.

Trying to put Martha's accusations behind me, I headed to the accordion doors of the children's section. I could smell fresh paint as I came to the closed-off area. There was a sign out front on a wooden easel announcing wet paint. I slid open the door and flipped on the light. The walls glistened with a fresh white coat. I jumped for a second when I saw a humongous monster that I recognized from the pages of *Where the Wild Things Are* perched in the corner of the room. That thing was so big it had to frighten small children.

The nonfiction section was near the back. I walked through the brightly colored beanbag chairs in orange, blue and green and searched for the nonfiction sign hung high on the wall. On one of the waist-high shelves was a large stuffed mouse perched on a piano bench sitting in front of a toy-sized grand piano. In front of this display was the book *The Mouse Who Played Piano*. The mouse and the piano were set up to look just like the cover of the book with everything but the lit candelabra. The children's librarian had probably decided it was too dangerous to light candles around the kids.

I took a step forward, still looking at the display, and then tripped over something on the floor. I scrambled off the object, and it took a second before I realized I had tripped over a *someone* lying on the floor. The candelabra missing from the mouse book display was placed on the back of a head of blonde hair. The person, a woman, was rolled over, face down on the carpet. I picked up the candelabra, checking to see if the person was conscious. I barely recognized Vanessa Markham from the streams of blood running down the front of her carefully made-up face.

"Vanessa." I shook her gently. "Vanessa, can you hear me? It's Betsy Livingston." Her eyes were open, but they didn't move toward me. In fact, they didn't move at all.

A scream shattered the quiet from behind me. Martha Hoffman stood with her trembling hands up to her mouth.

"You killed her! You killed Vanessa Scarlett!"

CHAPTER 10

In only twenty minutes, our author night at the library had changed from an evening filled with literary endeavors to an evening filled with criminal activity. Once Martha Hoffman screamed at me, most of the upstairs came rushing down to see what had happened. Being a policeman's daughter, I started dialing 911 and then tried to keep everyone back. Peter Markham came running in and grabbed Vanessa and held her in his arms. I noticed that Edith Martin, Damien Perez and Pattie had broken through to the front of the crowd and were now standing near the edge of the plastic curtain. Damien placed his hand over his mouth, and I heard him utter something under his breath. Edith, too, seemed stunned as she pulled her red shawl around her and shot a glance toward Vanessa's husband, Peter.

George Beckman was the first officer to show up on the scene. "Don't you worry, Betsy. I called Judd, and he's on his way," he said, putting his arm around my trembling shoulders. The crowd attending the lecture had been relegated back to the meeting room, except for me, Martha Hoffman and Peter Markham. After peeking over at the body, George began to tape off the scene from the folding door to the wall.

My father came in and ducked under the crime scene tape. Not wanting Danny and Zach to be around a homicide, he sent my Aunt Maggie to the parking lot, where the boys waited. She would drive them back to my house to wait for me. My dad surveyed the scene briefly and then came to me and took my hand. "Are you okay, Betsy?"

"I'm fine, Dad. I'm the one who discovered the body."

"What were you doin' in here?"

Martha Hoffman stood up. "That's what I'd like to know. This part of the library was off-limits to our visitors. When I noticed the sliding door was open and was attempting to close it, I saw Becky here leaning over Vanessa with the candelabra in her hands. She must have just finished pounding her in the head just before I arrived. We all know she had it out for our dear Vanessa."

"That is not true." My voice pitched into a squeal, probably not the best tone to use when claiming one's own innocence.

"Yeah, well do the police know you told her off in front of God and everybody in the mall and wrongly accused her of trying to ruin Pattie in the Creative Cooks contest?"

My father looked at me. Of course he knew. George Beckman's eyebrows raised a bit as he learned of my mall incident.

"The part about her trying to knock over Pattie's cupcake tower is true, and yes, I told her so," I said. "The part about me pounding her in the head with a candelabra is not true. I came into this section to find a world record book for the boys, and that's when I discovered Vanessa Markham."

My father took out a small pad and pencil from his pocket and faced the increasingly hysterical librarian. He scratched his head as he started trying to put the framework of the crime scene together. "And how do you know Vanessa?"

Martha Hoffman sobbed into a tissue. "This was Vanessa Scarlett, author of *Girl Meets Fifth Avenue*. She was the hottest author in Pecan Bayou."

My father wrote that down. "And she was most probably hit in the head with that little candlestick thing?"

Martha continued being the official voice of crime information. "It is the candelabra from *The Mouse Who Played Piano*. You obviously don't know your children's literature."

My dad grinned. "I obviously don't. I thought her name was Vanessa Markham."

Martha looked at my dad as if he were a rough-hewn barbarian. She spoke slowly to him, as she would to a small child. "This is Vanessa Markham, who writes under the pen name Vanessa Scarlett."

"I see." My dad went back through his list. "So let me get this straight, Miss Hoffman. You are saying you think Betsy here was responsible for killin' Miss Scarlett in the library with the candlestick?"

I stifled a giggle. It was highly inappropriate to laugh when a human life had just been taken. I heard another giggle behind me and saw Pattie trying to hide it in a cough. Whispers went up behind her as Ruby's crowd, who had snuck in behind Pattie, repeated the joke and then more muffled laughter.

Martha Hoffman's face turned a deep burgundy as the unintended joke registered in her brain. She walked over to Peter Markham and extended her hand. "Peter, I am so sorry for your loss and for you having to be around people like this. We will get justice for Vanessa."

Peter stepped slightly back from her and then answered in a whisper, "Um ... Thank you."

*****

After the two-man Pecan Bayou police department did its best to get the names and addresses of all of the people present in the library that evening, my dad and George sat down with me. Art Rivera, the county coroner, came in with a stretcher to remove Vanessa Markham's body. As he was wheeling the black body bag away, he stopped for a moment to ponder. "Miss Betsy, weren't you at the last murder in Pecan Bayou?"

He patted my father on the shoulder. "Seems to me, Judd, you and Betsy are a little overboard on that take-your-daughter-to-work thing."

"What can I say? She just keeps findin' 'em." As the coroner left, my father turned to me and spoke in earnest."Betsy, if you weren't my daughter I'd be taking you in. You have to look at the facts. You had an argument with the victim that was observed by others. Hell, you had an ongoing feud that was witnessed by half the town."

"That wasn't my fault, Dad."

"Sure," he said. "Then there's the sticky little matter of you holding the candlestick when Miss Hoffman the librarian came in."

"I was moving it so I could see if Vanessa was alive. I was not hitting her with it."

"You don't think I know that?"

"Miss Betsy," George said, "did you see anyone, anyone at all, leaving the children's section of the library?"

"No. Everyone was going upstairs for cupcakes. I was trying to get away from Martha Hoffman, who was accusing me of being the reason that Vanessa didn't make it to the author's night."

My dad checked his notes. "According to Miss Hoffman, this section had been closed off today because of renovations. She says the painters left at around four-thirty this afternoon."

"So how did Vanessa Markham and her murderer get in here?" I said.

George rose from the tiny chair he had been trying to sit in and walked over to the plastic divider. "Lieutenant Kelsey, do you think someone could have walked into the library and snuck into this room? All they had to do was unlock this latch."

My dad stood up and walked into the main part of the library. "What about the people who were out in this part of the library checking out books? It would have been pretty tough to sneak in here." He turned back toward me, scratching his head. "I know you were having difficulties with the woman, but do you know if she had any other enemies?"

"I saw her fighting with her husband at the Pecan Bayou Gazette."

He reopened his notepad. "What were they fighting about?"

"Sounded like she caught him cheating on her."

"Did they drop a name?"

"Nope."

"Okay, that gives us a start," he said.

"Oh, and I saw her getting pretty cozy with Damien Perez in the mall," I added.

"Why does that name sound familiar?"

"*Camazotz Chronicles*," George said, his voice in awe. "Those are some pretty powerful books. Bella and Edward may be hot in this country, but the Mexican Camazotz are really scary."

"Huh?"

"Damien Perez writes vampire books," said George.

"Oh, that hooey." My father gestured as if sweeping George and his Mexican vampires out of the air. I continued.

"Well, maybe they were just real good friends, but he seemed pretty hot under his pointy black collar."

"We'll check that out as well. Art will be calling me in the next couple of days, but we're pretty sure it's going to be blunt-force trauma. I guess I don't have to tell you to stay in town."

"I'm not much of a flight risk, Officer Judd."

After being dismissed by the police, I went back to the meeting room to retrieve my things. Pattie offered to stay until I was finished with my interview and then drive me home. She sat there looking at the copy of my book. Martha had straightened out the meeting room and returned the table to the center. I hoped Martha Hoffman had given up on the idea of an author's night.

"Are they all done grilling you?" Pattie asked.

"Funny, coming from the cookbook writer," I told her. We gathered our things and started walking toward the door. I waved at my dad and George as they were bent over their work at Pecan Bayou's newest crime scene. Once we were out the door, Pattie looked back and whispered.

"I thought I was going to die when your dad started in on the Miss Scarlett-in-the-library thing."

"I know what you mean. Why is it sometimes when a person is at an intensely somber moment, something just tickles them and they have an irresistible urge to laugh?"

"I don't know why we laugh at times like that. Maybe we've just held it all in for so long, we can't stand it and something triggers our goofy side. It's an awful thing, but I always feel better afterward."

"I felt really bad, snickering in front of Peter Markham," I said.

"Me too, but when I looked his way he seemed ... distracted."

"Yeah, I noticed that too."

We stepped up into Pattie's pink-and-white striped delivery van. As I settled myself in the seat, I could smell the lingering aroma of fresh baked goods. My cell phone rang inside my purse. It was Fitzpatrick.

"I've been trying to call you, Betsy. I was thinking about our weekend."

"Sorry, I left my purse in another room," I said. I debated at this point whether or not I should tell him I had discovered yet another body.

"Are you at home?"

"No, sorry. I just left the library, but I'm heading that way."

"You're just leaving? Your meeting must have run late."

"Well, it sort of did."

"Betsy, I make my living predicting incoming storm systems. Is there something you're not telling me?"

"Maybe."

"Betsy?"

"Okay, okay. I accidentally discovered another dead body."

It was quiet on the other end. Somehow, being romantically involved with a woman who had a knack for finding dead people was maybe a little on the strange side.

"Do you want me to come down?" His voice was so gentle I caught my breath.

"No," I answered, my voice hoarse. Pattie pulled up to my house, where I could see the living room light softly glowing through the window. "Listen, I'm home. Can I call you tomorrow and tell you all about it? I need to go see about Zach."

"Sure ... and Betsy ..."

"Yes?"

"Be careful, okay?"

"Okay."

Pattie was smiling, "Who was that?"

"That was my friend from Dallas."

Pattie recalled our earlier conversation about my debate over spending the weekend. "Oh, *that* friend from Dallas. He sounds like a nice fellow."

I jumped down from the van, shut the door and turned to the open window. "He's very nice. He was even nice after I told him about finding a body tonight."

"Why wouldn't he be?" she asked.

"You're right. It's not like it's my fault or anything."

"At least that's what you told the police," Pattie giggled.

"Come on, Pattie, you know I didn't do it."

She smiled. "You silly, I know – but I don't think Martha Hoffman does."

CHAPTER 11

"Are those waffles I'm smellin'?" my dad asked as he came through the back door to my kitchen the next morning.

"Why yes, I think your deductive reasoning is right on target," I answered, pouring batter into my waffle iron. "I wasn't expecting you for breakfast."

"I know, but I had some things I needed to talk to you about, and I figured it was better to talk to you here than down at the station."

"Oh." I put the metal lid down to let the waffles begin cooking. Zach came shuffling out in his floppy-eared puppy slippers and bright red pajamas dotted with the escapades of super heroes.

"Hi Grandpa," he yawned, sitting down at an empty plate. The sun shone through the white kitchen curtains fluttering in the morning breeze. I got the "World's Greatest Grandpa" mug out of the cupboard and poured a cup of coffee. "Black with two sugars."

"Thank you darlin'," he said as he took a chair next to Zach. We enjoyed a quiet breakfast of waffles, syrup and juice while Zach and my dad talked about their next fishing trip. When Zach left the table to dress for school, I started cleaning up the dishes.

"I wanted to let you know that because you're my daughter and a suspect in the biggest case to hit Pecan Bayou in awhile, Chief of Police Wilson will be taking the lead. He's worried I may not be totally objective in finding Vanessa Scarlett's murderer."

"Afraid you won't turn your own daughter in. That's reasonable." I rinsed off a sticky plate and put it in the dishwasher. "When Arvin Wilson starts checking on Vanessa, he's going to find out she had two sides. One was the beautiful and poised side our community saw, and the other was low down, mean and dirty. She was absolutely driven to be the first and best at everything, at any price."

My dad sipped his coffee. "Come on, Betsy, she didn't look all that mean to me. Crumpled up there on the floor of the library, she looked a little sad."

I sat down at the table. "I agree, she did. But in the last two weeks I saw her tangle with just about everybody she came in contact with. I know I shouldn't have reacted the way I did, telling her off at the mall, but she destroyed Pattie's entry and then blamed it all on Zach and Danny. You know you can say all kinds of things about me, but you go blaming my kid ..."

"I know, Mama Bear, I know." My dad chuckled and patted my hand. "I feel the same way about you. If I didn't, I wouldn't be riding shotgun to Chief Wilson."

"I think the deeper you dig into Vanessa's background, the more people you'll find who aren't all that sad she's gone."

"Could be, but this morning I'm going to visit with her biggest fan, Martha Hoffman."

"Good luck with that."

*****

There was a memorial service for Vanessa Markham on Thursday. All of the writers from author night were sitting in one pew at the Pecan Bayou Community Church in the same order they had been told to sit in at the library. As I walked toward them, Pattie scooted over and tapped the pew so I could complete the set. Damien Perez leaned over Pattie and said, "Good morning, señorita."

"Good morning," I replied.

"You are done with the police?"

"Probably not, but they seem to be satisfied for now."

"Good." He turned back toward the front of the church.

Pattie pointed to the other side of the aisle, where Martha Hoffman was dressed in a black cardigan and skirt and held a lace-trimmed hankie up to her nose. "Seems she didn't want to sit too near us. You know she's been sharing with anyone checking out a book how you clobbered Vanessa right there in the children's section."

"Wonderful," I whispered. Martha glanced over at the two of us and then jerked her head back when our eyes started to meet. I would have to make an effort to console her after the funeral just to watch her squirm.

In the front row sat Peter, his head in his hands. Next to him was Rocky Whitson and two people I assumed to be Vanessa's parents. They were not what I had expected. Her mother had stringy blonde hair that hung straight to her collar. Her father was a burly man wearing a plaid shirt under a dark suit that looked a little small. I wondered if it was borrowed. It explained a lot about Vanessa's drive to look better than anyone else in the room. Her parents didn't look like bad people – they just didn't look like Vanessa.

As the pastor spoke of Vanessa's life and achievements, I saw her mother's head bend as she quietly cried into a tissue. At one point, Peter looked back at our pew with a wistful expression. Perhaps he was acknowledging our presence, and it was his way of thanking us for attending.

After the final hymn was sung we were dismissed to the narthex of the church, where the ladies of the congregation had prepared red punch and cookies. We stood around balancing chocolate chip cookies on white paper plates, our discussions in somber whispers. Peter Markham was making the rounds, talking to all of the little groups clustered around their cookies. When he came to our group, he stood between Edith and Pattie.

"I just wanted to thank you all for coming today. I know some of you only knew my wife for a short while and I appreciate your show of support today."

"Of course," said Edith.

"Very sad," said Oscar Larry, taking little nibbles of his cookie at the same time.

Peter nodded in agreement to the obvious. "I just wanted to let you know, with Vanessa gone I'll be selling the house. I feel the need to make some changes. Vanessa had a pretty extensive collection of books on writing that if any of you are interested in, please come by the house." So was he here to thank us for coming or to tell us about the fire sale at his house?

"That is so kind of you," said Edith. "I already have so many books on writing, but your wife's fiction had such promise, I'm sure she probably had some good resources."

"Yes, I'm sure she did," said Damien, looking into his cup of red punch, his eyes not daring to glance directly at Peter's.

Pattie shot me a glance. We knew all about Damien's appreciation of Vanessa's resources.

"After I sell the house, I'll be moving in with a friend in Andersonville. I've had an offer to write for a community paper there."

"What about the investigation?" I asked.

"What about it?" Peter answered.

"Don't you have to stick around for that?"

"The police think Vanessa was killed during the afternoon hours on Tuesday, and I have an alibi. I was doing a play-by-play of a baseball game at the high school. I am anxious to find out who did this to my wife. I know Vanessa was ..."

No one dared fill in that blank.

Not getting any takers, he continued, "Vanessa was ... difficult ... but I never thought she'd anger someone enough to get killed. It's a crazy world we're living in."

"That's for sure," said Oscar Larry. After three hours of showing us slides of little green men, he would know about people being at the end of their ropes.

Edith Martin reached out and placed her hand on Peter's arm. "If there's anything we can do, please let us know. Anything at all." Peter's eyes moistened. "Thank you, Edith."

"Do they have any idea who might have done this?" asked Damien.

Peter glanced at me and then back to Pattie. "I've heard a few ideas of people, but at this point they really can't be sure."

"I ... really ... admired your wife," Damien said, his voice rough.

Peter cocked his head to the side in surprise. "Did you know my wife?" Oh boy, was that a loaded question.

"Just professionally, Mr. Markham, Damien said, looking at his watch. "My apologies, I am late for a meeting with my publicist." Damien offered his hand, and Peter shook it. Would he have shaken that hand if he had known that Damien and his wife had been involved? Peter had been so busy with his own affair he hadn't even noticed that Vanessa was having one of her own. If secrets were tennis balls, the church narthex would be bouncing with a sea of yellow-green fuzz.

"I can't believe you actually had the nerve to come to this funeral."

I jumped to see Martha Hoffman standing behind me with a cup of red punch in her hand. "You are the prime suspect, and you have the gall to come in here where we are mourning her loss after you so cruelly put her down with my candlestick."

I began to wonder if that was just fruit juice in her punch. The librarian seemed to be a little free with her commentary this morning. What was even more surprising was who came to my rescue.

Peter Markham stepped in front of me. "Miss Hoffman, I appreciate your loyalty to Vanessa, but the police don't know who murdered my wife, and I would appreciate you not causing a scene at her memorial service."

"Really," said Pattie, putting her arm around my shoulders as if to protect me from Martha's verbal attack. "Kind of tacky, if you ask me."

"You would side with her, seeing as she stood up for your lousy cupcake platter at the mall. I got news for you, missy. Any idiot can stack a bunch of cupcakes on a plate."

"Miss Hoffman, you're distraught." Chief Arvin Wilson came over as the noise level in the group rose. He gently guided Martha Hoffman away from our group.

As they walked away, Martha continued her accusations. "Chief, I'm glad you came over. I got some things to tell you about Becky Livinson over there."

"I'm sure you do, ma'am. I'm sure you do. Can I drive you home?"

As they left the church, I felt obligated to address this with Peter. "Peter, you know I am just the one who discovered your wife's body. She made me angry, but I could never kill another person."

Peter Markham took a deep breath and put his hands behind his head. "Like I told Miss Hoffman, I'd like to take today to grieve for my wife. Nothing else."

"Of course," I said, feeling as big of an insensitive interloper as Martha Hoffman had been. I felt awful for bringing it up and tromping all over this man's grief. He drifted away to the next crowd of people.

"Don't worry," Pattie reassured me. "If you hadn't said anything, then Martha would have gotten away with accusing you of murder in front of all of the people who actually liked Vanessa. You had to speak up."

"I guess you're right," I said. "But if I don't figure this out, that woman is going to make sure I get the chair."

CHAPTER 12

A couple of days later I showed up on Peter Markham's doorstep. I really didn't want any of her books, but I did want to find something, anything, that could clear my name.

"Betsy," Peter answered the door in a wrinkled white polo shirt and what looked like a two-day growth of beard. His blond hair, which had always been so carefully groomed at the Pecan Bayou Gazette, was now pointing every which way, and the date of his last shower was questionable. I handed him a tater-tot casserole and gave him a little hug, holding my breath so as not to breathe in the smell of unwashed man. "How are you doing, Peter? You look a little rough."

He ran his hand through his hair as if he suddenly realized how awful he looked. "I'm okay." He gazed off and then jumped, probably realizing I was standing there staring at him. "Oh, let me show you to Vanessa's office where she did all of her writing. It's really just a spare bedroom but we never had children, so ..." He paused. "Let me show you the way."

For a guy who was cheating on his wife, he was a mess. You never know how much you'll miss a person until they're really gone, I guess. I was surprised how much I hadn't missed Barry. When he left I thought I couldn't live a day without him. Now if he came back into my life, I couldn't live a day with him.

We climbed the white-carpeted stairs of his two-story brick home, passing tasteful black-and-white photos of the two of them in a montage of activities. There was a picture from the beach, a picture of them playing football on what looked strangely like the Kennedy compound and a picture of what had to be the two of them on skis zipping down a hill. If you knew of this marriage just through these pictures, you would think everything was perfect.

Peter opened a white hallway door to a beautiful room with sunlight streaming in through white curtains patterned with thick green stripes. "This was her hideaway from the world." He paused as he scanned the room as if for the first time. "It seems so empty now." Was this the first time he'd opened the door to this room since Vanessa's death?

"Thank you, Peter. Are you sure you want me in here digging around through her books?"

"I don't know. I guess. I'm just going to box them up, anyway. I don't plan on writing any fiction, so this is just one more job I have to do in cleaning up the house to put it on the market."

"Alright, then. Why don't you go and have some of that casserole and maybe take a shower and relax," I hinted, knowing I wouldn't get any good digging done as long as I had Peter here.

"Great," he said with a blank stare. I nudged him, and he walked back out of the room toward the stairs.

Once he left I headed to the bookshelf and took out a book titled *Get Your Novel Together in 30 Days*. Yeah, right. That would be what I took out of here when he came back. I noticed most of the writing books looked new, like their covers had never been cracked. This would be quite a find for a new novelist. I hoped others would come and visit, or maybe they could use this collection at the public library.

I sat down at her desk. It was white with gold trim and delicate curving legs, and not very much storage. Below it she had a white fluffy rug and a gold trashcan. I opened the only drawer in the desk to find neatly aligned stamps, stationery and a very expensive Mont Blanc pen. Not much there. I lifted the keyboard on her desk and found a folded note. It was from Martha Hoffman.

I must speak to you. We can get away for a moment while the alien guy is talking. I talked to him on the phone, and it took me forever to get off. He'll hog the time for as long as we need.
—Martha

I remembered their little disappearing act while the rest of us suffered through slide after slide from Oscar Larry. Whatever they spoke of, Martha was not too happy when they returned. Then when Vanessa was murdered, Martha acted like it was her own daughter on the floor. What was that all about?

Leaning up against the bookcase was a white filing cabinet with lacy wood inlays. I wasn't even sure where you would find a thing like that. I opened the drawers to find a rainbow of multicolored file folders where Vanessa kept track of her writing details. She had files for book sales, schedules, and there were even some rough drafts of works in progress. As I pulled the drawer out further, I spotted a familiar pink-and-white striped box. So, old Vanessa was a closet cupcake eater. The box was empty except for the vestiges of some coconut and chocolate frosting. I opened the lower file drawer and found three more boxes hidden inside. Vanessa had a major thing for these cupcakes. Oh boy, I couldn't wait to tell Pattie that Vanessa wasn't buying all those cupcakes for her husband. How did she get away with eating cupcakes and staying so fit?

I went back to her bookcase. As I ran my finger along the books I found three books by Destiny Wood. Was Vanessa thinking about writing romances, or did she just like a good bodice-ripper now and again? Maybe she was curling up on that couch with a romance in one hand and a cupcake in the other. When it came right down to it, she was more like the rest of us than she let on.

I noticed there weren't any pictures of her parents in the room. Had she been ashamed of the two people I saw at the funeral? Had she ever visited them? Had she let them visit her?

At the lowest shelf of the bookcase was a brown wooden box turned sideways to resemble a book. I pulled it out of the shelf, and a stack of letters fell to the floor. I could hear the microwave beeping downstairs and figured Peter was heating up my casserole. I picked up the scattered letters. Unfolding one, I read:

My darling, I cannot wait for another opportunity to be with you. Your lips are like satin ...

Okay, I got the idea what kinds of letters these were. At the bottom of the letter was the name Damien with the D finished in a beautiful flourish. She didn't seem to need too much time with Edith's books. She had her own personal bodice-ripper. Hearing a dish clank below, I stuffed the letters back in the box and replaced it on the shelf. Maybe I should be kind and take the letters away so as not hurt Peter. Then again, it really wasn't any of my business whether or not he read those letters. I sighed as I debated what to do; he just seemed so fragile at this moment.

Peter would be up those stairs shortly, so I looked around the room one last time. She had some magazines scattered on a table by her bright green couch. Most of them seemed to be about nutrition, which made sense when you thought about how in shape she was. Maybe she was reading about ways to exercise off excess cupcake calories. "Lose 10 pounds in 10 days!" "You Are What You Eat!" "What Junk Food Retailers Don't Tell You!"

"Did you want some of her magazines, too?" I jumped a mile as Peter stood in the door with a bowl and spoon. He took a bite. "Delicious."

"No, thank you," I said. I reached over for the book I had picked out earlier. "But this book looks great. Very helpful." I started for the door. "Thank you so much for giving me this opportunity, Peter."

"No problem. Oh here, why don't you take this nutrition stuff she started collecting. There's a couple of cookbooks in here and a bunch of other stuff." He handed me a pile from the corner of various books about cooking. Maybe there was something in there I could use for my column. "Hey, tell Rocky I'll be in tomorrow to clean out my desk," he continued. "I hear he's got some new guy in covering sports. It's some high school senior working for peanuts."

"Well, there's not a lot of guys around here like you, Peter. You were a real asset to our paper. I'm sure Rocky hates to see you go."

"Yeah, but it just doesn't feel right to stick around here anymore. I have a friend who's in ... another town." He looked down into his casserole. "I guess you heard our fight that day, so I can't really hide it anymore. You know I wasn't faithful to my wife. It was so exciting at the time, but now that she's dead, it just feels ... flat. What kind of a schmuck am I cheating on somebody who then gets brutally murdered?"

"So are you going to her?"

"I guess so, if she'll have me. I'm not too sure if she wants me now that I'm not attached, and oh, I was just questioned in the untimely death of my wife."

I squeezed his arm and started descending the white steps toward the front door. "Listen, I'm no expert here, but I did lose my husband suddenly and not under very good circumstances. Take a little time to find yourself first. I waited for years for my husband, and during that time I guess I slowly became who I am today. Heck, I'm still just starting to date after all of that. It's a tough adjustment to make, Peter. Whether or not your marriage was perfect, it being over is ... different." I juggled the books and magazines to open the front door, ready to make my exit.

"Thanks, Betsy." He put his bowl down and hugged me again, this time a long, long hug. I was afraid my face would be blue from holding my breath that long. "No problem, Peter," I answered.

As I felt Peter let go of me, a blue Toyota pulled into the driveway. Edith Martin, a.k.a Destiny Wood, climbed out of the driver's side.

"Well, hello, Edith. Have you come to look at Vanessa's books?" I said as Peter and I moved away from each other.

She walked toward us, her sandals making tapping sounds as each foot hit the sidewalk. "Hello, yourself," her reply was crisp. Nothing like the sweltering love scene I'd heard her read at the library. I guess you couldn't be in that mood all the time, even if you do write romance. She stamped up the walk and pushed by me without a word and started up the stairs before even asking where Vanessa's study was. Had she been here before? Maybe this was her second visit to come look at books. For a woman who had so many novels penned, I was surprised she wanted some other writer's books.

"Edith, don't be that way," Peter said.

Suddenly I understood. She had been here before, but not to look through Vanessa's library. She was the other woman. Why hadn't I put it all together before? Could it have been the fact that Edith Martin did not look like anyone who would have an affair with a man who looked like Peter Markham? The two of them were so very different from one another. Peter was a handsome young man in his early thirties and looked like he had come straight out of a Hollywood casting call. Edith was Edith. She was so much older, probably weighed around 115 pounds and just didn't exude anything that seemed too seductive. She was the kind of woman I would invite to my book club, not set up with a young single male friend.

Peter's face flushed, realizing what I had just figured out. "Betsy ... it's complicated."

I backed up, nearly falling off the stoop. "I think I just realized that. It's also none of my business, Peter. Thanks for letting me stop by."

As he closed his front door, I pulled out my phone. Pattie would just die to hear this one. I rang up the bakery, and she finally answered on the fifth ring.

"Pattie, I think I know who Peter Markham's other woman is."

I heard a cash register ring in the background. "Thank you," Pattie said away from the phone, then she spoke directly into the phone. "Who?"

"Try Edith Martin."

"What? You're kidding me, right?"

"I wouldn't have believed it myself if I hadn't just seen the two of them together."

"Where?"

"I was just at Peter's house, digging through Vanessa's study to try and find something to take the heat off of me. And you'll never guess what I found stuffed in the back of her bookcases?"

"What?

"Empty boxes of your cupcakes. There had to be four or five of them. And on top of all that she actually had magazines out about nutrition and the dangers of junk food."

Pattie laughed. "You never know who the closet cupcake eaters are, do you?"

"It was when Peter was giving me a hug at the door that Edith drove up and got really huffy."

"Like she thought ..."

"Like she thought Peter and I had just ... well she's the one with the vivid imagination in that area."

"Oh my gosh, Betsy. You're lucky you got out alive. Did you ever stop to think it might have been Edith who killed Vanessa? Now we know she certainly had a motive."

I heard the cash register jingle again and Pattie's thank-yous.

"I didn't think of that, but I can't believe it. Edith was upset with me today, but generally she's been pretty nice to me. Not like Martha Hoffman."

"Oh, you can never tell about people, Betsy. Even the nice ones."

After we hung up, I thought about Pattie's statement. Had Edith killed Vanessa out of jealousy? If she had, why would she not work a little harder to cover up her involvement with Peter? No wonder he showed up on the night she read her love scene at author night. Was he there to hear her fiction or to relive old memories?

CHAPTER 13

I needed to know what it was Martha and Vanessa had been discussing during the meeting, so I headed over to talk to the one person in this town who truly hated me. I checked the time, and Zach was at Little League with my dad for another hour. I could talk to Martha until she tried to drop-kick me out of the public library. Knowing this would probably require all my stamina, I pulled through our local coffee house, Earl's Java, and picked up a caramel macchiato.

"Hey Betsy, wanted to let you know, I loved your recipe for coffee creamers," Earl, the proprietor, said. "You're drinking one now."

"That's great, Earl. Did you make the mocha flavor, too?"

"Yes, but I added just a touch of cinnamon to mine."

"Yum. Well, this ought to get me through," I said. "Thanks, Earl."

"No problem, Betsy, and tell Judd his officers can drive through for a free java anytime."

"I will. Thanks again." I pulled out of the drive-through and took a swig of my coffee, feeling it rush through my bloodstream and stimulate dulling nerve endings. I pulled into the library parking lot and walked in under the shade of the large trees that surrounded the building. I walked through the entrance and into the main library.

Martha was behind the circulation desk, her high-backed stool squeaking as she entered data into her desktop computer. She had her glasses down on her nose as she squinted at the letters on the screen. She had on a crisp white blouse with a bow tied at the collar. She did not look up when I stood at the desk in front of her.

"No beverages inside the library. Take it out to the tiled entrance. You can pick it up after you check out your books."

"Oh," I said, taking one final gulp of the coffee and setting it down just outside the door on a table in the tiled area. When the carpet in the

83

library was new I remember them telling the kids to leave their muddy boots in this location during heavy rains.

I walked back to the desk and stood while Martha continued to type into her computer. Realizing I wasn't going anywhere, she finally looked up in exasperation. "Can I help ..." Upon realizing she was facing me, the killer of her dearest friend, her professional smile fell flat. "What do you want?" Ah, the real Martha.

"I want to ask you about this." I pulled out the folded note from Vanessa's office.

"Where did you get that? It's personal property."

"Well, I was invited to choose writing books from Vanessa's collection, and I found this little note folded inside of a book I took home," I lied.

"Fine." She reached across the desk to grab for it, but I was too quick and pulled it out of her grasp. She snorted. "I suggest you go home and do whatever it is you do. That issue is none of your business."

"Yeah, well as long as you are shouting out to anyone who will listen that I'm a murderer, it becomes my business. What was so important that you had to talk to Vanessa?"

"Nothing. Vanessa and I were very close. I don't expect you to understand. When you killed her, it's like you killed a part of me."

"First of all, I didn't kill her. Second, where do you get off talking about this special friendship you had? She just wanted to get that tacky book of hers into your library."

"Tacky book? That book was a masterpiece. I can show you the reviews."

"You have the reviews? Really?"

"Yes, I do. A book like that doesn't come along every day, and a local author that talented is hard to find. She knew her craft."

"I read her column in the paper. I wasn't all that impressed by her use of the word 'dashing' three times in one article."

"Poor editing."

"Give it up. She wasn't that good."

"So why did her book get picked up by a major publisher?"

"Because she looked so good on the back cover?" I said. How *did* she get a book accepted by a major publisher? Why was her book so good and her column so bad? I looked back at Martha, who seemed to be ready to dedicate an entire room of the library to her. Then it hit me. Martha wasn't protecting the memory of her friend, she was protecting her book. A book that Vanessa could have never written. If she didn't, who did?

"Miss Hoffman, you wrote the book, didn't you?" I said. For once, Martha Hoffman didn't jump back at me. She didn't say anything but toyed with a pad of yellow sticky notes on the desk for a moment. Finally, her eyes met mine.

"She paid me. Well, at first she paid me. She just thought it would look good if she was a columnist and a novelist. She tried writing a book on her own, but you were right. She wasn't very good at writing ... anything. Her emails were atrocious. So when she offered me money to write for her and then a percentage of the book sales, I agreed. I had always wanted to write a book, any kind of book. I could be a fashionista for money. I wrote it in four months, and then Vanessa started submitting it with her picture and her column on her writing resume. She got an agent and a book deal in less time than it took me to write the book. She was so beautiful – the publisher was thrilled to be able to put her on the back of their books." She picked up a newspaper that was folded on the circulation desk. "I mean look at this, even the vampire guy has a book signing at Petal's Books on Friday. Are his books any good? Who cares, what a great book jacket picture he takes!"

"So why did you need to talk to her at the meeting that night?"

"Because she stopped paying me. She told me to forget about ever seeing any more money for the book because now she was the one who was doing the work selling it, doing book talks, making the appearances. She deserved all the money and I was out."

"But she wouldn't have had anything to sell if you hadn't written the book."

"Damn straight," Martha said.

"What are you going to do now? The book is in her name, and all of the profits will go to her husband."

"I have a record of her emails, and I have my original manuscript. I don't know if that will work, but I'm going to try to sue for ownership. The thing is, once that publisher really sees who wrote *Girl Meets Fifth Avenue*, I probably won't get a second book deal."

Wow, we'd just had a conversation without her calling me a murderer. Surely she still couldn't believe I killed Vanessa. If anyone had a motive, she did.

"So who do you think killed Vanessa?"

"You."

"Okay, just checking," I said. "You're wrong, and I'll prove it." I backed out to the tile entrance and picked up my coffee. "By the way, have you told the police what you just told me?"

"I guess I will now. Oh, and one more thing ... I'm revoking your borrowing privileges."

Good old Martha. Mean to the last drop.

CHAPTER 14

I took a sip from my coffee cup and was thankful the brown cardboard liner had kept it pretty warm. Checking my watch, I still had almost an hour until Zach was finished. Maybe I would head over to the ballpark to watch Zach practice and talk to Dad.

So Martha was the girl in *Girl Meets Fifth Avenue*. Unlike dogs and their owners, writers do not often look like the protagonists they write about in their books. I pulled out of the library and headed toward Little League practice. I pulled up to the stoplight and turned some music on the radio. It must have killed Martha to see her book become a success and Vanessa take all the credit for it. If Vanessa cut Martha off, what did she plan to do about a sequel? Maybe she had herself believing she actually did write it herself.

The car behind me honked its horn. I had missed the light turning from red to green. That wasn't like me. I pulled through the intersection, and suddenly began to feel dizzy. Why were the streets so slanted? The street department had a lot of work to do in this part of town. What was that tree doing in the middle of the road?

*****

I woke to the sound of beeping in my ear. Something had to be wrong with my alarm clock, because it never used to beep like that. As my eyes started to focus, I realized I was not in my bedroom. I remembered something hard against my face. It felt like a steering wheel. Then I remembered being in my car, but as that thought came to me I realized I was no longer there. It was way too bright and white to be in a car. Maybe I was in heaven and the smoke alarm was going off. I wondered, why would they need a smoke alarm in heaven? Uh oh, maybe I wasn't in heaven.

"Betsy?" I heard my name being said, but I had no idea where the voice was coming from.

"Is that you, God?"

Then I heard God laugh, and he must have had some of his angels with him because I heard them laugh, too. "Betsy, open your eyes."

I pried my eyes open to see my father, Aunt Maggie and ... Leo Fitzpatrick? What was he doing here? For that fact, what was I doing here? Maybe I was still dreaming.

"Betsy, you're in the emergency room," Aunt Maggie said. "You had a car accident."

"I did? How?"

My father reached out and took my hand. "You ran into a tree just off of Main Street. It knocked you out cold."

I nodded dully and then tried focusing on Leo, who had been standing there not uttering a word.

"Am I in Dallas?"

"No, I'm in Pecan Bayou," Leo said. "I know you told me you were fine even though you happened upon a yet another murder victim. Let's just say I decided to act on my own just in case something like ... this ... were to happen. I tried to call to let you know I was coming down. When I couldn't get you, I called your dad. That's how I ended up here. You must have one heck of a headache."

Once he said that, I realized he was right. I did have a dull ache. I reached up to my hairline, where the ache seemed to be coming from. I felt a bandage.

"You hit your head on the windshield when your car hit the tree. The doc says you're a very lucky girl it didn't do more damage than it did or you really could be talking to God right now," my father said.

"I should have known when I finally got to heaven that God would sound just like my father." The room shared another laugh mixed with feelings of relief.

I jumped up in the bed. "Oh my gosh! Where's Zach? I was going to his practice."

"It's okay, it's okay," Aunt Maggie said. "Zach and Danny went down the hall looking for a vending machine. Danny wanted to buy you a candy bar because he says the smell of chocolate is the best way to wake you up."

"Did you have to leave ball practice?"

My dad waved his hand. "The boys were just about finished when I got a call from the department telling me you had just hit a tree. We packed up, and I called Maggie on the way."

I sat back against the pillows trying to pull together all that had happened in my brain.

"Why did I hit a tree?" I had heard about those cars with the faulty accelerator that made cars unable to stop. Had that happened to me? "Did something go wrong with my car?"

"Not that we can figure out," said my father. His tone became gentle. "Betsy, did you have anything to drink before getting in the car?"

"It was eleven in the morning. Of course I didn't have anything to drink." I wasn't that big of a drinker, and morning drinking just made me think of the kind of headache I was having right now. Did they all think I was out driving bombed out of my brain?

"Alright, alright, forgive me, but I had to ask," he said apologetically. "Your being unconscious is not so much the bump on your head, but you were passed out."

"Passed out? You're kidding, right?"

"Not kidding."

"Huh? That makes no sense."

"You sure you didn't have anything to drink?" Fitzpatrick repeated.

"No!" I said. "Wait." They all looked at me like someone in the middle of an intervention. "Wait. I did have something to drink. I completely forgot."

My father let out a sigh. "We thought you might have."

"No, it's not what you think. I had a cup of coffee from Earl's Java."

"Coffee? Was there anything in that coffee?"

"It was a caramel macchiato. That's all. The roughest thing in it was an extra Sweet'N Low." Aunt Maggie clucked her tongue at me.

"What? I like my coffee sweet, that's all."

My dad flipped open his cell phone. "George, go back through Betsy's car and see if you can find a coffee cup from Earl's. We're going to need to test that." He waited for a moment while George spoke. "No, she wasn't drunk, but she could have been drugged." He closed his phone. "By the way, your car has a dent in the front but is otherwise still running."

My father pulled up a chair next to my bed. "Betsy, I wasn't sure if I wanted to share this with you, but now I'm wonderin' if someone has made an attempt on your life. There's something I need to talk to you about."

"What?" I asked.

"It's about Barry."

"Barry drugged my coffee?"

"I didn't say that, Betsy. The other night when George called me about an old case, it had to do with Barry."

My father had known something about missing husband and hadn't told me? I couldn't believe it. He continued, "Now just hold on and don't get your dander up. I didn't tell you because I wasn't sure if it really was Barry. I had to check it out first."

"Had to check what out? Is he dead? Did you find a body somewhere?" That had always been the thing that Zach and I feared the most, although we tried not to talk about it.

"No, there wasn't a body, but after you hear this there might be one." I know my dad was making a joke, but I was already being investigated for one murder so it wasn't all that funny.

"So what are you checking out?"

"A marriage license." It was as if he had hauled back and slapped me in the face with the sting of his words.

"Barry got married again?"

"We're not sure. A Barry Livingston came up applying for a marriage license in El Paso. Of course, there are no picture IDs in applying for a marriage license."

"But he never signed off on our marriage. I divorced him out of abandonment," I protested.

"Yes, you did, and according to the state of Texas, you are divorced." He squeezed my hand. "Betsy, we don't even know for sure if this is him. The ages on the marriage license are 35 and 57. If it's him and the age does line up, he's marrying a much older woman."

"So why are you telling me this now? Here?"

"I don't know, but it seems like with the drugged coffee and all ... "

"You think Barry did it? Why would he? He doesn't care about me."

"Well, I've got some more checkin' to do. Just be careful."

I leaned back against the pillows, feeling my headache intensify. Was Barry still alive? What would I say to him if I ever saw him again? Would he want to meet his son? Would he want joint custody of Zach? Things were a whole lot easier when he was a fuzzy shadow from the past. I wasn't too sure I wanted to have him back in my life again – not now, not ever.

CHAPTER 15

"Do you remember my old buddy Rusty Robinson who went over there to work with border patrol?"

"Don't tell me, let me guess. Barry is the only one trying to smuggle himself across the border the other way?"

"No, but he did find a Barry Livingston listed with a phone. He's living in an apartment there with this woman he's wanting to marry."

"Are they married yet?" I really was glad he was no longer a part of my life, but the thought of him marrying anyone else somehow bothered me too. Was he marrying someone who was as innocent as I was? Someone who had no idea what kind of man he was? Or was he marrying someone who was his mental match? Someone who could help him perpetrate whatever fraudulent activity he might be doing.

"Not yet."

"Do you know anything about her?" I asked.

"We're still checking up on her," my dad said. "Here's the thing, though, Betsy – have you ever thought about the fact that he owes you eight years' worth of child support?"

My head hurt as I touched the bandage once more. I really hadn't thought about child support. Things had been difficult for us after Barry left, and if I hadn't had the helping hand of my own family I never would have made it through. I hadn't known where Barry was. Deep down inside I thought he must have been killed somewhere, somehow. At first I thought he was the poor innocent victim of some random violent crime. After I found out how much money he owed and how he thoughtfully put my name on everything, if he was dead it was because he cheated somebody somewhere who wasn't as much of a pawn as I was. I felt anger rising up in my throat.

"I don't want his money."

My dad sat down next to me and took my hands in his. "I know you don't want it darlin', but what about Zach? He's going to be a teenager in a few years, and with that comes cars and insurance and all those expensive things teenage boys like to do. Then after that he's going to college. How much do you have saved in his college fund?"

He had me there. Zach's college fund at present was one silver dollar and a one hundred-dollar savings bond that would mature when he was twenty-five and probably finished with college. I sighed.

"I see what you mean, Dad. I still don't want his money. What happens if we do go after him for child support and now that he's paying for a son, he decides he really wants to have a son. What if he applies for joint custody? What if I have to share Zach with him, a con man and a cheat? What kinds of things will he teach my son? It just wouldn't be worth it. Zach can work his way through college. I'll take on another job if I need to, but letting Barry into Zach's life is not going to happen."

My dad took off his glasses and cleaned them with his pocket handkerchief. He usually did this when he was tired or frustrated with me. I knew he was realizing I was right about this one. He didn't want Zach in Barry's hands any more than I did.

"You've got a point there, darlin'. But you need to know that with police involvement, it may be something that's out of your hands."

"I know, I know. I have to hope that Barry abandoned us once and he'll do it again. He's known for years right where we are and hasn't done anything to try to get in contact with his son. We are a non-entity to him, that's all. I'm more than willing to keep it that way."

"Can we come in?" I heard Zach say from the hallway.

"Yes you can." I answered.

"Mom! You're awake!" Zach came barreling through the door and jumped up on the bed with me. Danny slapped a candy bar down on my lap and hooked his arm around my neck on the other side.

"I was going to wake you up with chocolate. That's how the Easter Bunny woke me up."

"Thank you, Danny," I said as he hugged my neck.

"Mom, your head looks bad," Zach said.

I reached back up where the bandage was. Here I sat, looking as bad as I possibly could with Leo Fitzpatrick standing there. Maybe he was rethinking that whole weekend idea. That, and the fact he thought I was a drinker. I looked over to him, now standing against the wall with his arms crossed. He seemed to be enjoying this whole scene with Zach and Danny.

I picked up the candy bar. "Chocolate does work wonders, Danny. Some people can't live without it."

"Uh huh," agreed Danny wholeheartedly.

"Would you like a bite too?"

"Uh huh." Danny grinned. I broke off a couple of pieces for him and Zach.

"Okay, let's let your Cousin Betsy get some rest," my father said. "According to the nurses station they'll be checkin' Betsy out by this evening. Now that she's sobered up." He grinned.

"Dad!"

"Just kiddin', darlin'."

"Leo, once she gets checked out I'll leave it up to you to get her home," my father said, with just a touch of menace in his voice. "Man-speak" for get her home safely and don't let her hit any more trees. Finally my dad left the room, leaving Fitzpatrick and me alone. Leo put his hands in the pockets of his light khaki pants and walked closer to my hospital bed.

"So maybe it was a little much for me to just show up. Sorry about that."

"It was a surprise."

"I just got this feeling about you being down here, and well, I did rescue you from a burning building once," he said. I did recall him carrying me out of a building, but at the time I wasn't sure he hadn't set the fire. Here he was again, but this time instead of being unsure of him I felt comforted by his presence. He took my hand in his. "How do you get yourself into these messes, Betsy?"

"I'm not looking for trouble, but it sure seems to be able to find me," I answered.

"Were you friends with this woman you found dead?"

"She was another blogger at the paper, and for some reason we didn't get along."

"What about her husband? Did you know him?"

"He worked at the paper, too, so yes, I knew him. He's a nice enough guy, but he was fooling around on his wife."

"Maybe that's why she was so hard to get along with."

"There's more. She was fooling around too, with a vampire writer."

"A what?"

"You know, a guy who writes stories about vampires."

"I really don't get what the fuss about vampires and their love lives is all about," he said. That was something else we agreed on.

"Well, this guy is really sexy, and I saw him and Vanessa together at the mall."

"What were they doing?" Fitzpatrick asked. He must have figured it out, because I started blushing.

"Oh."

"They were all over each other that day, but then she brushed him off," I said.

"Maybe he kept leaving little teeth marks in her neck?" Fitzpatrick said. As I laughed, I felt my skull rocking with pain again and had to stop.

"Have the police questioned him? A disgruntled lover is never a happy guy and often a prime suspect."

"I don't know. I'm not even sure how much they know about all the partner-switching going on in that marriage."

"You do know you are still the one they think did it, right?" Leo asked.

"Yes, I do." I looked at the standard-issue hospital clock on the pale green wall. Today's still Saturday, right? Damien Perez is doing a book signing at Petal's Books, here in town. I could go talk to him."

"Don't you mean, *we* could go talk to him?"

"Okay. How long are you here?"

"I have twenty-four hours, and then I have to get back. I left Mrs. Alvarez there with Taylor, but we've had some twisters along the Panhandle that I need to keep track of. Work gave me twenty-four hours to check on you and get back."

"Do the girlfriends of weather forecasters feel abandoned during hurricane season?"

"Pretty much," he answered. "I'd rather predict one than be in one. But I'm here with you for now, so let's make the most of it." I suddenly noticed he had drawn closer to me during our conversation. Very close. He leaned in for a kiss, a sweet kiss appropriate for someone coming out of a drunken, maybe comatose, state. It was nice. I reluctantly pulled away and asked softly, "Was making the most of it talking to Perez or kissing me?

His voice was hoarse as he said, "Let me call a nurse and see if we can start working on exit paperwork."

CHAPTER 16

We walked into Petal's Books about an hour later. It was an old building that had been modernized with pleasant tan siding. It had big picture windows that were always beautifully decorated for every season. Right now, the windows were filled with spring flowers and books with pink and blue covers. I spied Pattie's pink-striped book in one of the displays. I would have to remember to tell her about it.

Petal, who was the daughter of two flower children, had chosen the location for her bookstore very carefully in the downtown area. Her store was on the end of the street, right next to the city park and playground. Every Saturday she would ring a ship's bell she had mounted outside her door to announce story time to the children playing in the park. It was a wonderful idea, and she made a lot of money doing it, too. She also had a poetry reading night, political meetings and coffee always on. Petal might have been the daughter of free spirits, but she also believed in a free economy. Her husband was my accountant.

Damien Perez was sitting at a small table near the door, speaking to a couple of teenage girls who were clutching his red-and-black book and giggling. "Well, I hope you enjoy the vampires, girls," he said. They giggled again and turned abruptly, nearly knocking Fitzpatrick and me down.

"Betsy?" said Damien Perez, eying the bandage on my head. "What happened to you? Did someone come after you with a candlestick?"

"No, they slipped her a mickey," Fitzpatrick said, extending his hand to Damien. "I'm Leo Fitzpatrick, a friend of Betsy's."

"How do you do," Damien said warmly, shaking his hand. "So, did you pass out and fall over?"

"No, I crashed my car into a tree."

"Oh, my ..." He shook his head from side to side. "Unbelievable. This town is a dangerous place for writers."

"Not until this past week. I was wondering if we could ask you about Vanessa."

"I know as much as you do about her murder," Perez sighed.

"I know that, but I wanted to know about your ... relationship with her before the murder."

"Before the murder? You must be mistaken."

"Mr. Perez, I saw you and Vanessa in the mall last week."

Perez leaned back in his folding chair and touched the tips of his fingers together. I could tell he was deciding just how much to tell me. When he brought his chair back down to the floor, he looked back to Petal's location in the bookstore. She had gone into the back room. He began speaking in soft low tones. "We were lovers. We were together for almost six months, and then she ends it." He tapped his heart with both hands. "She broke my heart," he said, rolling the "r" in heart.

"How did that make you feel?" asked Fitzpatrick.

"How do you think it made me feel?" he said. "I was angry. In all my life no one breaks it off with Damien Perez. I am the one who finds the door first. It was humiliating." For a moment he forgot to keep his voice low as emotion overtook him. Was I hearing hurt, or was it anger?

I stood with my arms folded, listening to him. Damien took it as a judgment. "Ah, but I did not kill her if that's what you're thinking, my happy hinter."

"Well, you certainly had motive," I said.

"I had about as much motive as you did, and I'm insulted that you would think I would kill anyone. I am a gentle man. I do not kill."

Only in fiction, I thought. You not only kill, but you drink their blood.

"Besides, I saw the UFO man leaning on her car as we left the first night. Perhaps she had moved on to ... how do you say it? E.T.?"

That was news to me. Oscar Larry, the world's most boring man, was waiting for Vanessa? One thing this whole experience was teaching me was that opposites do seem to attract. Peter and Edith were proof of that. Maybe Vanessa had moved on to Oscar Larry or maybe he was upset about something she had done or said, just like so many others sitting in the library that night.

An hour later we were back at my house, where Aunt Maggie had thoughtfully put together some chili from the scrounged ingredients in my cabinets. She was just pulling some cornbread out of the oven as we walked in. I could hear Danny and Zach in the den with cartoons in the background. All of a sudden the idea of eating a bowl of chili and going to bed was pretty appealing to me. I yawned and sat down at the kitchen table, where Maggie placed a piping-hot bowl of chili and a glass of milk. Fitzpatrick took the chair across the table from me, and Aunt Maggie set a bowl in front of him.

"Thanks, Aunt Maggie. I don't know what I'd do without you," I said.

"So don't start tryin'," she replied.

Fitzpatrick laughed into his cornbread.

"Listen here, little girl. You're the daughter I never had, and getting a call that you were in the hospital just about took a year off my life."

"Sorry."

"I still don't understand what happened."

"None of it's very clear," said Fitzpatrick.

"All I can figure is someone must have followed me, and when I put my coffee in the outer area of the library, they put something in it."

"I thought Judd always warned you to never put down an open drink, not in this day and age."

"I know, but the library?"

Fitzpatrick was already finishing off his bowl. My aunt did make some excellent chili. He swallowed a mouthful, then grabbed a napkin. "Did you see anybody come in?" he said.

"No, I had my back turned – but maybe Martha did. She was facing the door."

"If she had, do you think she'd tell you?"

"No, she revoked my borrowing privileges."

Maggie scooped up Fitz's bowl. "More?"

"No, that was wonderful. You should bottle that stuff."

"She can't," I said. "It doesn't stick around long enough."

Shouting started in the next room: "Am not."

"Are too."

"You're a silly head."

"You're a silly head."

"Uh oh. Sounds like a fight." I scraped my chair out from the table and went toward the noise in the den.

"What's wrong?" I asked.

"Zach is a silly head," said Danny.

"I heard that part," I replied.

"Danny doesn't want to break a record any more," said Zach.

"I'm tired," Danny moaned and threw himself onto the couch.

"But we can't stop now. We haven't broken any records," insisted Zach.

"I'm tired," Danny repeated, a little louder.

Zach growled in exasperation and started stomping off to his room. As he got to the door he turned for a parting shot, "Silly head!"

Danny went over to Aunt Maggie and hugged her around her waist. "I want to go home now."

"You sure you don't want to eat some chili?" Aunt Maggie asked.

"No, Mom. I want to go home. I'm tired," Danny said.

"Hope he's not coming down with something," I said. I reached out and ruffled Danny's hair. "I know how you feel. I'm feeling a little tired too." Danny stood at five-foot-three, a couple of inches shorter than my five-foot-five. I had been five years older than he was, and his development was much slower than mine, so we never played together like he and Zach did. Right now he and Zach were at the same developmental age. I wondered and worried how long that would last. Would Zach enter puberty and leave Danny behind? I guess we would find out in just a few years.

Maggie gave me a hug before they went out my back door. "Glad you're okay," was all she said, but from the tightness of the hug I knew she felt much more.

Fitz looked at his watch, "My twenty-four hours are almost up. Will you be alright tonight?"

"Yes, I'll be fine."

"Do me a favor and try to stay away from the body finding, tree hitting and all-around dangerous behavior, okay?"

"At least you started with 'try.' That's the best I can do. As long as I'm the one they think did it, I have to find out who really did it," I said.

"I know you do, but don't you have a highly experienced and qualified police professional in your family who is doing the same thing?"

"Yes," I admitted.

"So don't go all junior detective on us."

He reached out and pulled me in, giving me his own version of goodbye.

CHAPTER 17

On Sunday, after finishing my latest blog post about using dryer sheets to dust baseboards, I headed to the land of little green men in San Antonio. Zach was still pretty down after Danny had given up the pursuit of world records, so the idea of going to a store devoted to aliens helped to bring him around to his old self.

According to my GPS device, Oscar Larry's shop was right on Alamo Square. What would the original fighting men of the Alamo have thought if they walked into the structure they so ardently defended to find it surrounded by shops, restaurants and tourists? Remember the ... T-shirts, posters and tasteful gifts for your loved ones! Not the same, I thought.

As we entered the busy store, Zach's eyes grew big as he came face-to-face with a life-sized alien doll. It was standing by the door holding a sign that said "Greetings." "Cool," he said, now spinning around as he took in alien T-shirts, books, DVDs and games. Up on the wall next to the register was a flatscreen TV playing a documentary about the discovery of alien life forms in Nevada.

Oscar Larry was not at the register, so we walked into a second room of the store. It was Sunday afternoon, after all. Maybe I should have called first. The inner room was a large area with bookshelves lining the walls, filled with what looked like hundreds of green and silver items. The other side of the room had rows of chairs and a video screen for presentations. Oscar Larry had probably bored thousands of people with his endless slides. Over in the corner stood Mr. Larry with his arms crossed and his thumb tapping at his chin as he listened to a small man adamantly telling him a story. He held up his hand to stop him.

"That is not what I told you to do! I wanted the pop-out aliens right there at the front door."

"Sir," the little man said, pushing up his glasses, "don't you think that might be a bit frightening for children who come into the shop?"

"All the better!" It seemed the mild-mannered alien researcher was pretty demanding with his clerk. Is that how he ended up first on the program and then chose to ignore the time limit?

What kind of name was Oscar Larry? Was Larry really his last name, or had he just dropped the last part of his name and stuck with first and middle name? Another mystery of the universe.

Today Oscar Larry wore a T-shirt on his thin frame that featured the familiar lime-green alien head with "Resistance is Futile" written around it. He recognized me as we approached him. He patted the short man on the back as if to dismiss him and turned toward me and Zach. "Well, hello. You're one of the authors from Pecan Bayou. It's Becky, right? So nice of you to come over and see my shop. I could tell just by looking at you that you had a heart for alien investigations." Oscar looked down at Zach. "Is this your son?"

"Yes, this is Zach, and my name is Betsy, not Becky."

"Oh, my apologies, Betsy. What do you want to see first?" He gestured to encompass the entire store.

"Could I look at that video game over there?" Zach said. There was a small game set up for customers to play while in the store that had caught Zach's electrical gadget fancy.

"Certainly!" We went over to the game setup on the counter. Oscar Larry reached behind the counter and produced a high stool for Zach to sit on while he played the game. Zach started pushing buttons, and Oscar showed him how to shoot down asteroids and aliens with great skill.

"This is great, Mom!" Zach said.

"Thanks," I said to Oscar Larry. "I was wondering if I could ask you some questions."

"Of course! That's what I'm here for. Have you had an encounter or perhaps you're accounting for some missing time? Don't be embarrassed, you'd be surprised all the stories I've heard."

"I'll just bet you have," I agreed, "but my questions have more to do with the murder at the library."

He straightened up. "Oh. I know very little about that."

"Had you ever met Vanessa before the author's night?"

"No, not really. I had seen her column in your local newspaper."

"Really?" I was a little surprised Oscar Larry had taken the time to read a column about fashion, but I guess men were allowed to be interested in fashion, too.

"It's not what you might think. I approached the editor of the Pecan Bayou Gazette – what's his name, Shifty?"

"Rocky."

"Yes, right, Rocky. I wanted to write a weekly column about UFO sightings in the Texas area. I am constantly being told stories by people coming to visit the Alamo. It would have been a wonderful sharing of insights and information about the subject matter that I hold dearest. Unfortunately, your editor did not share my enthusiasm and chose to include that woman's fashion blog instead." He stopped talking for a moment and fingered a small rubber alien on the counter, rolling its little head between his thumb and forefinger.

"After reading the drivel she wrote, I was understandably angry. Who really cares about a new handbag line compared to life on other planets?"

My thoughts exactly. "So how do you feel about my column?"

"At least your column is useful to people. By the way, I read your column about digital coupons and used your advice here in the store. We put one up on the website for glow-in-the-dark alien putty. We sold out in a week."

"So who do you think killed Vanessa?"

"It wasn't me. Frankly, I was pretty sure it was you," he said, putting the little rubber alien back in its cardboard box on the counter. "The more time I spent around her, the more I found myself disliking her. This whole shop is built around alien encounters, but also fears of something that is unknown, hidden and possibly dangerous. Most importantly, these things are real. Vanessa Markham was not. She was all about the appearance of something, a show. Even with all that, I felt sorry for the woman, and well ... there is an opening at the paper again, now isn't there?"

Would Rocky include this guy's column right next to mine? I could just see it in the latest addition, Betsy tells you how to get that stubborn stain out while Oscar Larry talks to you about getting that troublesome alien to stop popping out of your chest cavity.

"Did you ever speak with Vanessa?" I pressed.

"Yes, just briefly before the night I spoke to the library audience. She made some derisive comments about my work. I'm not proud to tell you I returned the favor and called her a shallow, hedonistic idiot."

"Nobody told me that."

"We were quite alone at the time, and I would appreciate that being kept quiet."

He could appreciate all he wanted but a fact like that needed to be in the hands of the police.

He continued, "Besides, you had words with the victim as well. I'll bet if we lined up every person there that night with a beef of some sort with Miss Vanessa Markham Scarlett, the line would have stretched around the block."

"You may be right about that. I know I didn't kill her, but trying to find someone who *didn't* have a motive is getting pretty tough."

"Well, scratch me off your list. I am interested in life, alien or otherwise." Oscar Larry then noticed his clerk dragging an alien display across the room and abruptly ended our conversation. "No! No! Not on that side, we already have the alien autopsy photos over there."

Was he right? Was he too busy with his business to murder Vanessa? How much did he really want that column? Was it enough to kill?

*****

As Zach and I pulled up into our driveway later that day, I recognized Edith Martin's car. She was sitting in the front seat tapping away at a tablet computer and promptly snapped the deep red cover closed when she saw us. As she opened her car door to get out, I noticed a pink-and-white striped box from PattieCake's. Today she had on a denim skirt and multi-colored geometric knit top that showed off her slender, if not downright bony, form.

"What a surprise," I said, noticing the scowl on her face.

"I needed to speak with you," she said.

"So you drove all the way over from Andersonville? I'm surprised you didn't just call me."

"I didn't have your number, and I used this as an opportunity to stock up on baked goods from your friend Pattie's bakery." In the backseat there had to be a dozen boxes of cupcakes. Edith caught the look of surprise on my face and quickly cut me off. "They freeze beautifully. I find eating a cupcake is a terrific writing aid for me. You know, chocolate imitates the feeling of falling in love. It is very helpful to be able to reproduce that feeling on a regular basis for the type of literature I produce." Looking at the backseat I could predict a chain of thirty books on the bestseller list for old Edith. She was quite the consumer.

Zach came out of our car playing with a little green plastic flying saucer he had begged for at Oscar Larry's shop.

"Won't you come in?" I said.

"That's not necessary," she cut me off. "Peter tells me there is nothing going on between the two of you, and I just wanted to make sure you feel the same way."

"I know what you came up on that day, but truly, I was just expressing my condolences and he hugged me. That's all."

"Good."

"So you and Peter are out in the open now about your relationship?"

"Why not. She's dead now. No reason to sneak around any longer."

"Aren't you worried the police will question you about your motive?"

"Possibly, but I didn't kill her, and that's all they need to know."

"Um, how did you and Peter meet?" I asked.

"Don't you really want to ask how did an old lady like me get together with a pretty boy like Peter?"

I paused a moment. She was right. I did want to know, but it was nosy of me to ask right out. "I was curious about that," I admitted.

"I'm ten years older than Peter."

I raised my eyebrows as I mentally did the math.

"Okay, I'm fifteen years older than Peter," she admitted. "We met two years ago when I attended one of my nephew's football games. That was the year they went to state, and he had mistakenly put another player's name in my nephew's position. I went to the paper to complain, and we got into a long discussion about high school football in this area. I have always been an ardent football fan, and when my nephew started playing I went to every game. We started seeing each other at the games and discussing the plays. You know, football talk. He was not my type, and I clearly was not his, but we were both so comfortable with each other, it just worked. Slowly a romance developed out of that, and before you go imagining, it was nothing like what I write about in my books."

That was a lot for her to fill me in on, and I was worried she would share more with Zach still standing there swooping his little flying saucer up and down making circles around us.

"Well, as long as we're clear on who Peter is involved with, I'll be going," she said.

"You don't need to worry about me," I replied. Zach buzzed up to us. "Mom's got a boyfriend. Mr. Fitz."

Edith brightened up at that. "Good to know, young man," she said and hopped into her car and rolled her hand out the window to signal me to get the hell out of her way. The world of romance writers was a little too heated for my taste. I decided it was safer to stick to my own little dreary world.

What would have happened if I had told her I was involved with Peter? How would she have reacted? Was she capable of murder? She seemed quite pleased to be out in the open about her affair with Peter. I knew I needed to check in with my dad to find out how much he knew about all of these people and their crazy love lives.

CHAPTER 18

On Monday, Aunt Maggie asked me to pick up a special birthday cake she had made for Danny's twenty-fifth birthday. He loved the teen musical "High School Hijinks," and Aunt Maggie had asked Pattie to design something that looked like it.

An early spring day was one of the best kinds of days in Texas. The wildflowers were blooming in shocks of blues and purples all over the town of Pecan Bayou. Tourists were pouring in on the weekends to see the flowers, and money was pouring into the registers of the local merchants, Pattie included. During wildflower season Pattie kept her shop open seven days a week; she barely had time to restock the baking ingredients to make all of the delicious concoctions she created. I stepped into her pink-striped bakery and once again found myself behind a group of people ordering at the counter. Two women stood behind the crowd, and I stood in line behind them.

"Well, you know what I heard?" I couldn't help overhearing whatever this woman had heard. "I heard all those writers were lovey-dovey with each other doing God knows what, and one of them got jealous and boom! End of story, if you know what I mean." The other woman laughed at the joke. "All lovey-dovey" wouldn't be the terminology I would use when describing Vanessa Markham's way with people around her.

"You know the woman who runs this bakery was there."

"Really?"

"Oh yes, she was in on it just like all the rest. Now when we get up there don't let on that we know she was a part of ... well ... whatever happened in that library."

The other woman nodded in a hush-hush manner, clutching her pocketbook to her ample chest. "Makes me want to check out all my books online."

The two women approached the counter, where Pattie greeted them warmly and started filling their bakery box. Unable to contain her curiosity, one of the women blurted out, "We hear you were at the library the night that woman was killed."

Pattie didn't even blink an eye. "Yes ma'am, I was. Can I get anything else for you today?"

Not to be cut off by Pattie's manner, the woman continued. "Did you see anything or hear anything? Anything at all?"

"Sorry to disappoint you ladies, but I'm in the dark about the whole murder. Didn't hear or see anything until my friend behind you found the body. The cops think she did it. Came right up on the body without a sound. She's standing behind you, you know."

The two thrill-seekers jumped and turned around to face me. I smiled and nodded in agreement. The woman with all the questions grabbed the box and grabbed the other woman by the arm, pulling her out of the bakery.

Pattie and I laughed. "Oh my gosh, you should have seen the looks on their faces when they realized they were surrounded by whatever it was their imaginations were pondering," she said.

"It was pretty funny. Nothing like being notorious in this town."

"You got that right. So are you picking up your cake?" Pattie said.

"Yes, Danny will be so excited to see it. He started reminding us about his birthday last week. Like we could forget."

Pattie went into the back room case to get Danny's cake. I eyed the chocolate cupcakes in the case and tried to fight off the cravings. It took about thirty seconds before I gave in.

"Pattie, could you get me one of these chocolate cupcakes?" I said when she returned with Danny's cake in a pink-striped box.

"Certainly, and for you it's on the house."

"You probably don't want to start extending credit to me when we're talking chocolate," I said.

Pattie's door opened and I turned, expecting to see another crowd of people in for their baked-goods fix. I was surprised to see Oscar Larry heading toward me instead of the counter. He wore another alien-oriented shirt, probably from his own store. This one was a smiley face with two little antennae poking out of the familiar yellow circle.

"Mrs. Livingston. I took the liberty of calling at your home but you were not there. I was going to ask Pattie if she might know where you would be, but here you are."

"What can I do for you Mr. Larry? Did you drive all the way from San Antonio to see me?"

"Yes and no. I drove over here to see if I could get Mr. Whitson to include my column in the Pecan Bayou Gazette. I am rather thrilled that it has been up in two other community papers, and I would love to add Pecan Bayou Gazette to my list of publications."

"I thought you already had this conversation with Rocky."

"Yes, I did but that was before ... "

I was confused. "So why did you need to see me?"

Oscar Larry put his hands on my shoulders and started steering me toward the door as if I were an errant child. "I need you to go to Whitson and tell him about seeing my presentation at the library. Once he hears how in-depth my research is, I'm sure he will pick up my column for distribution."

I took his hands off my shoulders. "Wait a minute."

"What?"

"What? What?" I couldn't believe I was being pushed around by this guy. Why would he assume I would even want to promote his work with Rocky? "You want me to go and pitch your little-green-men column to my boss. Mr. Larry, you didn't even ask me if I believed in all this ... alien stuff."

"Don't you? I certainly demonstrated to you the irrefutable truths of the history of alien landings on our planet."

Pattie shook her head at the counter. "There was a lot of history alright, but that doesn't mean Betsy here buys into it."

"Ladies, you have become privy to more information than the average American has been given permission to know."

"Mr. Larry, I'm sorry you came all this way," I said, "but I can't go fight for a cause I don't even believe in myself. If you want this job with Rocky, then you're going to have to go in there yourself and convince him of it."

Oscar Larry pursed his lips in a sneer. "I cannot believe you could be so ignorant, Mrs. Livingston. I obviously put way too much faith in your intellectual ability. Perhaps some of those things Vanessa Scarlett was saying about you were correct. You are useless to me."

Oscar Larry turned on his heel and slammed out the door, shaking the pink and white stripes on the valance.

"That guy needs to go back to Area 51," Pattie said. "You went to San Antonio?"

"Sure. I seem to be the one the town is blaming for this crime, and I just wanted to see if maybe he could lead me to something."

"I'm amazed," she said. "Have you talked to anybody else?"

"I've talked to everybody." I answered.

"So Sherlock, whodunnit?"

"If I knew that, I could get the police investigation off of me."

"So you continue to be the fabled person of interest?"

"Oh yeah," I nodded.

Pattie handed me my chocolate cupcake on a napkin. "This might help," she said. I accepted it and sank my teeth into the smooth, creamy icing of one of Pattie's heavenly cupcakes. It was out of this world.

CHAPTER 19

Monday night we celebrated Danny's twenty-fifth birthday at my Aunt Maggie's house. She lived on top of a hill in a dark red brick cottage-style house. Zach handed Danny his present, the latest recording of "High School Hijinks the Musical." It was to be part of the entertainment tonight. Danny was so excited he hugged his cousin until Zach's eyes started to bulge. I took Danny's cake to the kitchen, where my aunt was scurrying about with paper plates and napkins. I volunteered to carry out a bowl of potato salad to the table.

Danny was horsing around with two of his buddies from Haley Village, where he worked two days a week as a waiter in their tea room.

"Betsy! It's my birthday!" He rolled off the words one by one. Aunt Maggie followed me in and placed Pattie's beautiful birthday cake in the center of the table.

"Alright, you hooligans!" my aunt shouted over the noise. "All of you go into the living room and jump around in there for a few minutes while we finish putting dinner on the table." One of the parents of Danny's guests helped to usher them into the next room. My dad came in with a platter of grilled cheesy dogs, Danny's favorite food. He set it down and put his arm around my shoulders. "How is my little prime suspect?"

"Dad, that is not funny."

"I know, I know. And you should know, as long as I'm in that office your side will be heard."

"As a matter of fact Dad, I wanted to talk to you about some of the other people who were there that night. Did you know about ... "

"The fact that half the people on that panel were sleeping with each other?"

Maggie dropped her cake-serving knife on the table.

"Uh, yeah, that's about it. Peter was sleeping with Edith, and Vanessa was sleeping with Damien Perez."

Aunt Maggie butted in between us. "Who was Martha Hoffman sleeping with?"

"No one," I answered.

"Could have called that one."

"But she ghost-wrote Vanessa's book and was being screwed out of the deal by her."

"Oh my."

"We got most of that information during routine questioning already, darlin'."

"Did you know Oscar Larry hated Vanessa because she beat him out for a job?" I said.

"That's a new one."

"He wanted to write a column for Rocky and lost out to Vanessa. He actually came to Pecan Bayou to find me. He wanted me to go to Rocky and tell him how wonderful his presentation was. When I refused, he was not too happy with me."

"Now that concerns me, because if he is the murderer, what's to stop him from hitting you in the head with a candlestick?"

We heard a roar come up from the other room.

"Sounds like the natives are getting restless out there."

"Dad, who do you think did it?"

"Can't say Betsy, can't say," my dad said as he stepped back, arms folded, surveying the well-grilled cheesy dogs.

"Because you know and don't want to tell me or because you don't know and don't want me to think less of your detective skills."

"I guess you'll have to find out on your own." His crooked smile told me he was finished revealing investigative tidbits.

Aunt Maggie put her hands on her hips and took a breath. "It all looks great. Pattie did a great job with Danny's cake. I could have never made a cake like that in all my days."

"Sure you could," I said. "Me, not so much, but you can do anything, Aunt Maggie." Maggie reached over and covered my hand with hers. "So can you, baby girl. So can you."

The evening was wonderful with cake, ice cream, cheesy dogs and a boisterous, if not ear-splitting, singalong with those kooky kids from "High School Hijinks." Some days, life is just too good.

*****

The next morning as I was driving to the Pecan Bayou Gazette, "The Eyes Of Texas Are Upon You" rang on my cell phone. I juggled to get it out of my purse.

"Betsy, I'm glad I got you on the phone. We've had some news about Barry."

I took a deep breath. Here it was, the thing I had been waiting on for more than seven years. From the tone in my father's voice, it didn't sound like this was going to be good news.

"What about him?"

"Okay, now don't get too excited. Promise me that."

"Yes, Dad. I am calm and collected. What about Barry?"

"The police talked to him down in El Paso. They took his prints, and they matched up with our Barry."

I felt a crunching inside of me. I knew it was the same feeling people described when someone they loved very much died. I had that feeling, but it was because the life I loved very much would now and forever be changed. Barry was alive, and I really didn't want him to be. Everything was so much more comfortable when he was this phantom husband who left and would never return. What would this do to Zach? If he found out, he would instantly want to meet him. He would put him on a pedestal, seeing him as the dad he had always envisioned him to be. Zach was just a child, and there was no way he could understand what a snake his own father was. The pain in my chest was quickly moving to my head.

"Betsy? Betsy, are you there?"

"Yes, Dad. I'm here. You're sure? You're absolutely sure it's Barry?"

"Fingerprints don't lie. They are questioning him on some possible fraud involvement down there, but as a favor to me, they convinced him they might be a little more lenient if he settled the mess he left up here with you. George has gone to get him."

Barry was coming back to Pecan Bayou – and with a police escort, no less. There was no getting out of this now.

"When will he be here?"

"They ought to have him here by Wednesday. If nothing else, there's the matter of back child support and making sure the two of you are good and divorced before he moves onto his next victim. It's time he closes the book on the two of you properly."

"Just another hazard of falling in love," I said. Had Barry been living under an alias? I knew whoever he was marrying was probably pretty. Barry liked pretty women, and he liked to be seen with them. He had always envisioned us as part of the country club set. Me, a cop's daughter? What was even funnier was that the country club set of Pecan Bayou was not exactly what I would call the elite. It was just the people in our town who liked to play golf and who could take the heat doing it.

"There's just one more thing, Betsy, and this is going to be tough to hear."

I knew this was one of those times when I would want my phone to cut out before he could finish the sentence. Darn these modern cell phones. I could hear him now.

"Okay. Tell me," I said.

"I spoke to Barry on the phone."

"I'm surprised he would even talk to you, Dad."

"I was too. The first thing he asked me was if Zach turned out like Danny."

That jerk. Barry had been terrified after a test came back indicating there was a possibility of Down Syndrome. He was never comfortable around Danny and was just sure we would also have a son like him. I always knew that the test was the reason that Barry split. He could handle the pressure of committing a crime, but he sure couldn't handle the idea of having a son who was less than perfect. On top of that, the fact that he might have a wife who would produce a child like that? Time to leave.

"What did you tell him?"

"I told him Zach was perfect."

I started to feel the crunching inside me again. Perfect? The one word I would have never used. Barry didn't need to know that the son he so feared was one of the most beautiful human beings God ever put on this earth. I knew now that Barry would want Zach.

"You told him he was perfect? Dad, how could you?"

"He is perfect. Barry needs to know what a great person he dumped and ran away from. He needs to feel guilt for what he did to you and Zach. I don't think he ever looked back. It's time he sees all he gave up."

"Don't you see Dad?" I said. "Now he's going to want Zach. He's a greedy man, and the idea of guilt just doesn't register with his brain. Why else would he be able to cheat people? He wants things he never had to work for, and our Zach has just fallen into that category. I was the one who fed him, changed his diaper, stayed up all night with him when he was sick. I was the one who did all the dirty work of parenting. Now he's going to show up here and try to take him. He's going to want custody of Zach." My voice broke as the tears came rushing in.

"I know, darlin'. But why would you think he would ever get custody? What judge in his right mind would give over custody to a father that once abandoned his son?"

"You never know, Dad, you never know. What if Barry decides to give his life to God or something? What if he starts up a soup kitchen or donates his kidney? He's a con man, and you would be foolish if you thought he wouldn't think of custody of Zach as his ultimate con."

"Okay, okay. Just settle down, Betsy. We're a family, and we'll deal with this together. Nobody is going to take Zach. Especially not this two-bit hustler."

I caught my breath. "Promise?"

"I promise."

CHAPTER 20

I went into the Pecan Bayou Gazette to turn in my column on dryer sheets. I had brought in Vanessa's nutrition magazines, thinking to take them down to Pattie after I finished at the Gazette.

"Putting in some new recipes? The readers love recipes," Rocky said as he walked by.

"No, these were Vanessa's. Peter gave them to me. I thought maybe Pattie would like them."

"Good idea. Say, would you like to do me a little favor and clean up the rest of Vanessa's stuff over there? Peter told me to do what I wanted with it, and if you hadn't noticed, I'm a little short-handed around here right now."

"Sure," I answered. I walked to the desk she had used whenever she had written her column there. I like writing my columns at home and emailing them in, but I guess Vanessa had wanted to be near Peter. Now whether that was to be close to him or to keep an eye on him, I would never be sure. She had a red plastic file box where she was keeping her research and columns. I looked through her alphabetical index to find articles on designers and invitations to runway shows. She also had a small black leather book that turned out to be a calendar. I paged to the dates before her murder. She wrote most of her things in a jagged form of penmanship, but I could make out most of it.

The week before the first library night, she had two appointments with D (Damien) and one appointment with Xavier in Houston. Was she having two affairs after hopping all over her husband for having one? The fact that she spelled out Xavier's name while only using an initial for Damien told me that she didn't care if someone saw his name on her calendar. Maybe Xavier was a designer. That certainly sounded like the name for one.

"Find anything of use to you?" I jumped as I realized Rocky was now standing behind me.

"I was just looking at her appointments the week before she was murdered. Do you know anyone named Xavier?"

Rocky stroked his chin and thought for a moment. "Nah, when she was in here she was always on the phone to somebody or another. It could be any of those people. She just called them 'sweetie' all the time. What a phony that woman was."

More than you know, I thought. I searched further in her box to see if there was a phone book inside, but feeling around the bottom I couldn't find anything. I knew asking Peter for her cell phone would be a little on the nosy side. Besides, my father probably already had it.

I pulled out my own phone, intending to call him about it, when it rang in my hand. The caller ID read Buzz Aldrin Elementary School. It was only 10 a.m., so this couldn't be good.

"Mrs. Livingston? This is the nurse at Buzz Aldrin. I'm calling because your Zachary is here in the nurse's office. He has an upset tummy and needs you to come and pick him up." The nurse spoke to me as if I were four years old and was merging over into baby talk.

"I'll get my things and be right over."

"Thank you, Mrs. Livingston. Zachary threw up in his classroom trashcan while reading the part of the second Billy Goat Gruff. We just think he was excited about getting to stand up front with the others."

"I'm on the way."

I picked up Zach at school and hurried him home, just in case he needed to throw up again in the car. With the major dent in it from the tree, I guess a little throw-up wouldn't do much more harm.

"Is the stomach flu going around at school? Have other kids been sick?"

"No, not all. I must be the first one," Zach answered.

"Did anybody at the party yesterday complain about being sick?"

"No. Not until after we ate, anyway."

"After we ate?"

"Sure, after we ate those cheesy dogs. Those were really good, Mom. Can we eat those every week?"

I remembered Aunt Maggie had sent a few cheesy dogs home with us last night. They were a little heavy on my stomach, but she thought maybe Zach could eat them.

"Wait, Zach, how many cheesy dogs did you eat last night?"

"Just one."

"Oh, okay. I thought maybe you ate too many and they made you sick. That cheese inside can make them a little heavy."

"I know, I know. This morning I grabbed a couple to eat while you were in the shower."

"You ate two cheesy dogs before you went to school? I thought you had a bowl of oatmeal."

"We were out, so I decided to take care of myself. Did I do a good job?" He looked at me, seeking reassurance for his grown-up can-do attitude.

"You did a great job." I sighed. Self-reliance had its price, it seemed. "Just, no more cheesy dogs."

"Okay." He hugged me. "Now can I have a snack? I'm hungry after throwing up in the trash can."

"You bet." When we got to the house I prepared him some toast. That would be light on his stomach until he had the cheesy dogs out of his system. I wondered how Danny was faring. You are what you eat, they say. I wouldn't want to be a cheesy dog. I took Zach the toast and then answered my ringing phone in the kitchen.

"Is Zach okay?" asked Rocky Whitson, calling from the Gazette.

"Yes, you don't need to stop the presses. He just had an overdose of cheesy dogs."

Rocky laughed. "Those things are nasty, poor little fella. Listen, I'm sending my new sportswriter over for some danish from PattieCake's. I'll go ahead and send over those magazines?"

"Oh, that would be nice, if he doesn't mind."

"He doesn't mind."

"Sounds like you have your hands full."

"I'm starting all over again. I never realized how much Peter did around here covering all the Little League, school league, bowling league ... What is in Andersonville anyway?"

"Don't you mean who?"

"Oh. You think I would have sniffed that one out. Ah well, time to share my wisdom with the kid."

That kid was lucky.

CHAPTER 21

After speaking with Rocky I sat down at the kitchen table with a legal pad, writing down everything I had learned so far about Vanessa Markham. She was on the outs with her husband, was cheating her ghost writer, was having an affair with Damien Perez, had angered Oscar Larry, was Edith Martin's other woman and had sabotaged Pattie's cupcake exhibit. She had pretty well pissed off the entire town at the same time. In the corner I doodled the name Xavier. With her penchant for exotic lovers, could she possibly be involved with another man? It was too exhausting just to think about. I dialed my dad's number.

"Dad, is there anybody named Xavier in Vanessa Markham's cell phone records?"

"Uh, let me look. She was quite a talker, that one." I heard paper rattling as my dad rolled through the names, "Damien, Peter, um ... here's an Xavier in Houston. Xavier Frank? Is that who you're lookin' for?"

"Yes, did you call him? Do you know who he is?"

"Um, yes we did call that number. Xavier Frank is a nutritionist."

"Really?" That went along with all the cookbooks and magazine articles, but it seemed a little in the extreme. Was she that obsessed with nutrition? Maybe she was getting ready to write a book about food. It had to be every fashion model's job to be in perfect physical shape. Maybe she was going to write a book to help the skinnies stay that way. Was she trying to create a sugar-free version of Pattie's cupcakes?

"Would you mind if I called him and asked him a few questions?"

"Betsy, I don't know if you noticed, but this is a police investigation. I just can't go handing out numbers to you willy-nilly."

"I know, dad, I know, but somehow I get this feeling that all of this is tying back to what she was doing days before her death, and that had something to do with this Xavier guy. Please?"

"Alright, Xavier Frank works for All Health Nutrition Centers in Houston. That's all I'll tell you."

"That's all I need."

"I know I don't need to tell you to not get yourself in trouble again, right?"

"Right."

"One more thing, Betsy. Barry arrives at the police station at around four tomorrow. I wasn't sure if you wanted to see him or not."

I wasn't so sure either. My emotional state anticipating our reunion ranged from excitement to disgust to terror. What do you say to a guy who dumped you and dumped on you at the same time? "I guess I'll see him," I said. I tried to make my tone light, knowing I probably wasn't putting too much over on old Officer Judd.

"You sure?"

"Sure."

"Good idea. See you then."

I hung up, feeling the dread creeping in. Why couldn't he have stayed hidden and out of our lives. Glancing back at the legal pad, I walked to my computer to search All Health Nutrition Centers on my computer. Zach had left his blue backpack on my desk chair when he came in, so I lifted it to put it on the floor. He had not properly zipped it up, and I could see the little journal his teacher had him fill out every morning when they first got to school. His journal didn't have a lot of words in it as much as pictures about whatever it was that was going on in his life at the time. I expected today's picture to be of Danny's party and the singalong. I leafed through the notebook until I found today's date scrawled in Zach's third-grade handwriting.

He had drawn a picture of me holding a candelabra standing next to a woman who was laying on the floor. He had taken a red crayon and filled in where he thought the blood would be. It terrified me to look at it. Did he think he think I killed Vanessa? Had I been so busy that I missed the fact we had had a murder happen and I hadn't taken the time to help my son navigate through the scary parts of it all?

I decided to wait on the computer search and walked into the den, where Zach was being mesmerized by various talking animals on the television. "Zach, I need to ask you something." He didn't move his eyes from the screen.

"Uh, if this is about that book report, I'm almost halfway finished with the book."

"Zach." Still no change in the direction he was looking. I picked up the remote control and turned off the TV. "Zach, tell me about this drawing you made in your journal," I demanded.

He looked at the paper slowly as if he were just seeing his own artwork. "Oh, that. Some of the kids told me about you finding the lady in the library. I didn't know they found you holding a candlestick over her.

"Who told you that?" My father, Aunt Maggie and I had been careful to shield both him and Danny from the gruesome details of the crime. Here it all was in front of me in living crayon color.

"The kids at school knew all about it. It was in the paper. Mr. Rocky wrote about it."

Thanks, Mr. Rocky. "I need to ask you something really important," I said. "I'm holding the candlestick in the picture, and it looks like I'm the one who hurt Miss Markham. Do you think I would do a thing like that?"

"No!" He sat up straight on the couch. "You wouldn't hurt anybody, Mom. I know that," he reassured me. "You just found her. You didn't kill her." He did quite a job at making me feel dumb for asking.

"Good." I took his hand. "I want you to know that because I was standing there, some people thought I was the one who hurt the lady. They are wrong, and you are right."

"You bet your ... " he stuttered, realizing what he was just about to say in front of his mother. " Uh ... you bet."

"Zach! Where did you hear that?"

"Grandpa," Zach answered simply.

"Grandpa. I should have known. Well, he may say it but you're not allowed to."

"Even after I'm as old as him?"

"Even then, young man," I said as I exited the room. I was relieved to know my own son didn't think I was a murderer. I was not happy to know I was the subject of the gossip at Buzz Aldrin Elementary. I placed the journal back in Zach's backpack and zipped it up.

Sitting at the computer, I looked up All Health Nutrition in Houston and started dialing the first of three offices. I found Xavier Frank at the second office.

"Mr. Frank, this is Betsy Livingston in Pecan Bayou. I knew Vanessa Markham and was given the responsibility of cleaning out her desk at the Pecan Bayou Gazette. I noticed you were on her appointment calendar just a few days before she died. If it isn't too personal, may I ask why she was meeting with you?"

"Miss Livingston, it really was a personal matter between the two of us."

Had I been right about her being involved with yet another man? "I'm sorry if this is none of my business. I just assumed this had something to do with all of the research she had been doing on nutrition before she died. I didn't realize that it had to do with ... something else."

"Something else?" Mr. Frank stopped for a moment. "Oh, something else. No ma'am. I'm a happily married man, Miss Livingston. It was nothing of that sort. No, not at all. She simply brought me some food she wanted me to analyze for its nutritional content. She was very conscientious about what she put into her body. I wish more people were like her. Heart disease and diabetes in this country would become a thing of the past."

"Did she mention that she was maybe writing a cookbook or a book about nutrition?"

"If she was, she didn't mention it to me." I heard a phone buzz in the background.

"Forgive me, Miss Livingston, but if that's all you need I have another call."

"Thank you for your time, and if you should remember anything else ... "

"I have you on my caller ID," he said.

So Vanessa had been interested in nutrition but hadn't told Xavier Frank why. So who knew? Her husband? Her lover? Her ghost writer?

CHAPTER 22

After an uneventful evening working with Zach on his book report, I sent him off to school the next day healed from the perils of cheesy dogs. As I settled down to work at my computer, I heard the gravel in my driveway crunch and looked out to see a white sedan coming to a stop. When the driver's side door swung open, I recognized the face of Police Chief Arvin Wilson.

He wore a tan straw Stetson, a white shirt and a navy sport coat. He looked a little older than his 60 years, probably because of his hefty frame. A tiny cigar dangled from his mouth as he came up my steps. He stubbed it out on the porch and tapped on my door.

"Hello, Betsy," he said. "I wanted to ask you a few questions about what happened down at the library last week."

"Certainly, come on in." He stepped over my threshold and took off his Stetson, revealing thinning gray hair. I motioned for him to come into my kitchen.

"Am I still a suspect?" I asked as we sat down at the table.

"Let's just say you are a person of interest." Always the diplomat.

"Have you looked into all of the other people she had ticked off in the week before her death?"

The chief smiled. "There does seem to be quite an extensive list. Can you tell me about the exchange you had with her at the Pecan Bayou Mall where you were competing in a ... " He opened a little black notebook like my dad carried and then pulled out a pair of black reading glasses. "A cooking contest?"

"Vanessa was always very competitive, and we were pretty sure she pulled out one of the leg supports on Pattie's display, making herself the winner by default. Pattie had by far the best creative cooking there,

128

but once her table collapsed she was out of the competition. Vanessa blamed it on my son and cousin and ... we exchanged words."

"Who was standing there when the table collapsed?"

"My son and cousin."

"So she was correct?"

"She was and she wasn't. They leaned on the table, but she had set it up so that any weight on it would make it fall."

"So you say," he said, writing down my words.

"So I know." It was easy to see whose side he was on.

"Then you had another argument with her at the library?"

"She accused of me of making the whole incident up in front of all of the people waiting to hear the speakers in the library. What she was saying wasn't true." I felt the back of my neck heating up.

"How angry did this make you, Betsy?" he asked.

"Not angry enough to bash her in the head with a candlestick."

"Can you account for your whereabouts the afternoon before the second author's meeting?"

"Yes, I can. I was with my son. He was trying to break a world record. I left him with my father before I came to the meeting."

"And you never left here between the hours of 3 to 6?"

"Nope. Just ask Zach."

"And how old is he?"

"Eight."

*****

As the morning progressed after Chief Wilson left, a feeling a dread rushed over me. Did I need a lawyer? Could this really be happening? I started looking through my address book heaping with business cards I had stapled onto the pages. I jumped when Rocky Whitson knocked at the door. I didn't even know he knew where I lived.

"Hi Betsy, can I come in?"

"Sure. Is everything alright?"

"Oh, um, well ..." he stammered

"Come in." He pressed on the squeaky handle of my back screen door and then placed his hands in the pockets of his brown corduroy pants. I pulled a chair out for him at my kitchen table.

"We just received word of a letter that was left at the library for Martha Hoffman. It was a threat against her life."

"You're kidding. Too many library fines?"

"Betsy, I'm being serious, now. The letter was pretty graphic about how somebody was going to do in Miss Hoffman before the week was out."

"Do you think this is somehow connected to the Vanessa Markham killing?"

"Pretty sure of it."

"Why? Do you think it might be from Vanessa's killer?"

"I certainly hope not. It was signed by you ..."

"By me?" I interrupted.

" ... and Martha Hoffman is dead."

"She's dead?"

"They found her just an hour ago. Your dad was busy with the crime scene and asked me to come and talk to you. She was killed at her house, strangled with her own bathrobe belt. It looks like whoever killed her, she let into the house. There was a second note at her home, signed by you."

"And the note said I killed her?"

Rocky tried to remain calm, probably in effort to keep me calm. This was becoming a nightmare. It seemed like more and more things were happening and happening to me. "Yes, they found the note on her desk in her home office. It was typed, but signed by you."

"That is the absolutely stupidest thing I've ever heard," I said. "If I was going to murder someone, I sure wouldn't leave a signed note."

"Well, the police would tell you that people who murder other people aren't always the sharpest in the knife drawer," Rocky said.

I grimaced. "Strangled. Martha Hoffman was never nice to me. She never got my name right, and she belittled what I do for a living, but she didn't deserve that." This also proved to me that whoever killed her also killed Vanessa and was now using me as his or her scapegoat.

"What were you doing last night? Do you have an alibi?"

"Last night I was here with Zach," I said. "He was recovering from cheesy dog poisoning, remember?"

"Can you prove that?"

"Sure, Zach can tell you."

Rocky drummed his fingers on the table. "What about after he fell asleep?"

"First of all, I would never leave my child alone, and second, I didn't do it."

"I'm just saying these are the questions the police will ask you."

*****

Two hours later, I found myself sitting at a gray folding table in the Pecan Bayou Police Department across from Arvin Wilson.

"So you're saying you didn't send this letter?" Wilson asked.

"Uh, no. If I were going to threaten to kill someone, do you think I'd be dumb enough to sign the letter?"

"I have no idea what you might be dumb enough to do, Betsy."

I heard a knock on the two-way mirror behind the chief and could pretty well tell that had to be my own father.

"Listen," said Chief Wilson, now getting exasperated having to deal with a real case and a real suspect, "I want to believe you, Betsy. For goodness' sakes, you're the daughter of one of my best men, but every time I turn around this case leads me back to you."

"I didn't threaten Martha Hoffman with a note, and I certainly didn't kill her," I said.

"But you did have an argument with her just a few days ago."

"Yes, and then someone put something in my coffee cup after Martha told me to place it out of my own reach. What about that one? I ran into a tree and ruined my car. I didn't see you dragging her in on that one."

"She was questioned about the matter. But that makes you angry because maybe you don't feel like she was given the same treatment as you?"

"I didn't write that note. For some reason, somebody is setting me up to look guilty. Maybe the killer wrote that note because I was your main suspect anyway. What a way to assure not being caught – pin another murder on me. Have you thought about that?"

"Let me read the note to you," he said:

Dear Martha,

I know you put a sedative in my cup the other day. For that you must die. If you don't think I can do this, then you are wrong. You'd better keep an eye out behind you, Martha dear. You're dead.

"How do you keep an eye out behind you?" I asked.

"Is this your signature?" The chief pointed to the bottom of the note. It sure looked like I signed it.

"Sort of."

"So you admit to writing this note?"

"Nope, and until you can prove I wrote this note, this interview is over." I rose from the table and was greeted at the door by my father. He took me by the elbow.

"Thanks, Arvin. From here on out Betsy will be sharing information with you through her lawyer. Just to be on the safe side, you know. We'll have the handwriting expert from the county check out the signature. I'm sure it will show it isn't Betsy."

My dad propelled me toward the outer door of the police station. "Good job in there, Betsy," he said. "You need to know that innocent people have been known to go to jail in Texas and have ended up with a death sentence. We need to work fast and smart to find out who is setting you up."

We walked out of the police station into the beautiful midday sun. The air felt thinner and cleaner out here somehow.

"We'll get you out of this darlin', I promise."

CHAPTER 23

As we started for my car, George Beckman pulled in to park in front of us. I couldn't believe my timing. Barry was sitting in the backseat.

I had rehearsed what I would say to Barry for the last eight years, but right now I found I was at a loss for words. I think I knew more what I wanted to do than say, and it wasn't give him a basket from the Pecan Bayou Welcome Wagon.

George Beckman got out of the car, stretched and then opened Barry's door. As he pulled him out of the car by the elbow, he smiled and they chatted as if they had been buddies on a long car trip. Barry came out and looked up at the building, shading his eyes from the sun. He looked so different from the handsome young man who had walked out into the night so many years ago. He now had a dark brown beard. It was well trimmed, but his hair had thinned some on the top, taking away some of his boyish look. His midsection was just a little bit thicker than the well-toned abs he had left with. George held him by the elbow as they came up the stairs to the glass doors. I stood back, the pressure of my father's hand the only thing keeping me from screaming out what a bastard I thought he was.

Barry passed by us on the steps, and when his eyes met mine, he immediately looked down. The joking manner he had shared with George suddenly vanished. He didn't want to look at me. He didn't want to talk to me. He just wanted to walk on by and forget I even existed. That is what he did best, after all.

"Hello, Barry. Glad to see you finally got back. How's that cold of yours?" I said. He had told me he had a terrible cold and was going out for cough drops. I had no idea the closest drug store would be in El Paso. Barry didn't answer me at first but then turned to George. "I don't have to talk to her. Put me in my cell or whatever it is this podunk police department has."

"This podunk police department has a state-of-the-art holding cell that'll keep your ass for as long as we need to." My dad's anger was rising.

"You got nothing on me, old man."

"Try abandonment, back child support and Lord knows what else you've been up to in your business dealings."

"Did you get notified about the divorce?" I asked.

"Who cares?" he sneered.

"Now Barry," said George, "don't be rude. Betsy here was just asking you a question."

"I still don't have to talk to her."

His words hurt. This was the real Barry. This was the kind of guy who would leave a pregnant wife with a stack of bills.

"You son of a bitch." I started toward him and felt my dad pull me back. Chief Wilson came out of the police station and registered surprised seeing me again so soon and yelling at somebody else besides his murder victim. "Is there a problem out here, Lieutenant Kelsey?"

"No, no problem, Chief. I would like for you to meet my ex-son in law, Barry Livingston."

The chief grabbed his gun belt around his round middle and smiled and extended a hand. It wasn't until Barry put out his hand that the chief noticed he was being escorted by George. He pulled his hand back.

"We're looking at him for some fraud charges here in Pecan Bayou," said my dad.

"I see. Well, as long as everything is okay out here."

"Fine, just fine."

Chief Wilson stepped back into the building.

"Where's the kid?" asked Barry. He finally had something to say to me, and it was about the one thing I had left that he could take away.

"The kid's name is Zachary, and if I have it my way he will never lay eyes on you."

"Oh, yeah? If I have it my way I will take rightful ownership of MY son."

"That's enough," my father said. "Thanks, George. I'll take your prisoner from here. Why don't you head over to Benny's Barbecue and he can fix you up with a hot meal on the police department." George tipped his Stetson and turned back to his car.

"Betsy. You head home now. I'll call you later." My father took hold of Barry's arm to guide him to the holding cell. Barry turned toward me and looked me up and down.

"You're still looking good, Betsy. What's this? No ring? Probably hard to find another man like me."

I felt my skin crawl at his appraisal. The last thing I wanted was another man like Barry. At least now I knew what I was up against. Now I knew – even more important than clearing my name for murder, I would fight to the end to keep my son.

*****

When I returned home, I wasn't sure what I wanted to do first – call a lawyer or go into the witness protection program to get away from Barry. I actually entertained thoughts of packing my car, picking Zach up from Aunt Maggie's house and driving off to God knows where to start a new life. He had done it to me, why not do it to him?

Deciding that might be a little too drastic, I called Rune Jackson, one of the five lawyers in town. I didn't have to tell him much before he agreed to take on my case. He had dealt mainly with DUIs in his career, and this was his first murder case.

"Listen here now, Miss Betsy," he drawled, and I somehow knew he was sitting there with his boots up on his desk, his Stetson pitched back on his head. "I don't have any legal assistants here, so I'll be needin' you and your daddy to help me check the alibis of all the other suspects on the day Martha Hoffman was murdered."

"I'm sure my dad has some of that already."

"Yes, but we need to check on our own as well."

Later, as I helped Zach get ready for Little League practice, I told my dad about my lawyerin' up, as he would say.

"That's good. Has he done any murder cases before?" he said on the other end of the cell phone.

"Nothing like this. He said we needed to help him to check out the alibis of the other people who might have killed her. I have to tell you, I don't want to talk to Oscar Larry again. Who knows what he'll do."

"I'll take care of him," my father said. "You go talk to Peter Markham and that woman he was running around with."

"The romance writer?"

"Oh, right. I guess that's fitting. I'll ask Maggie if she can go ask around at the library to see if there might be anyone there who was angry with Martha."

"Okay. I can talk to Pattie, too. I wanted to thank her for doing such a nice job on the cake."

My dad and aunt were doing it again. They were fishing me out of another mess. I might have my share of troubles, but I knew in that moment I was truly blessed with these two. "Thank you. Thank you for always being there."

"Betsy," my dad answered, "you stop this. You're not going anywhere." As I plopped a baseball hat on Zach's head, the steady reassurance of my father's voice seemed to soothe me. We could do this.

CHAPTER 24

After watching Zach drop balls for an eternal two-hour practice at the local park, we were back home again. I was between the proverbial rock and a hard place. My son's father was sitting at the Pecan Bayou jail. This was the man he had dreamed of meeting for years on end. Should I tell him about his recent appearance, or should I stay quiet about it for as long as I can? I was deciding on the latter when Zach came into the room freshly bathed and wearing pajamas.

"Mom, why are you staring out the window? Is there somebody out there?" Zach put his hands on the windowsill and leaned on the glass, smudging it with his nose. He smelled like strawberry bubble bath.

"Uh, no. There's no one out there."

"Then what are you looking at?"

Here it was, my opening for, "Oh, by the way, I ran into your father today." I fluffed his hair with my hand. "Nothing. Just day dreaming."

"You're too old to daydream, Mom. I thought it was only kids in school who did that."

"Speaking of school, is your homework finished?"

Zach's shoulders slumped. "Aw, mom."

"Get to it, buddy. Time's a-wastin."

Zach turned around and slunk back into the den, where he had a crumpled math paper still waiting for him on the coffee table. As he walked away I could see his similarities to Barry. He had the same dark hair, the same pale blue eyes, and sometimes I would see Barry in the way he would move his hands when he was telling a story. Those were the times when I once again saw the guy I had fallen in love with so many years ago. That man was dead to me now, replaced with the balding, bearded man who sat in my father's jail.

I had been trying to organize my notes on old columns all afternoon. I was due to return for another try at my on-camera NUTV appearance in only a week, and I was feeling plenty nervous about it. How would I demonstrate some of the stuff that I wrote about in my column? I couldn't exactly fix a sink or repaint a house. I had a database full of helpful hints, but the thought of sharing them with someone through a television camera was pretty scary. Maybe I would watch the home and garden channel and see how they did it.

I heard a faint tapping at the door and looked up. At first I thought it was Rocky returning to tell me someone else had been murdered and darn it if there wasn't another note with my name on it. I saw familiar pale blue eyes peering through the screen door.

"Betsy! I'm home ..." Barry's voice said, a la Jack Nicholson in "The Shining."

"What are you doing here?"

"What do you care? Where's my boy?"

"I'm calling the police, right now."

He came barreling through the door. "Zachary? Where are you, boy? Your pappa is home."

It was my worst nightmare come true. I was no longer in control of what Zach would know about Barry.

"Mom?" Zach came back out of the den but then stepped back when he saw the bearded man at the door.

"Zach, go back into the den."

"Mom, are you okay?" He looked at the man in the doorway and started to shrink back.

"It's me Zach. It's your dad."

Zach's eyes opened wide as he realized he was looking at his own father. "Dad?"

"That's right, son. I'm home." Barry put his arms out for Zach to run into them. To Zach, though, he was still a stranger. He looked to me for guidance. I walked over and held his hand tightly.

"Zach, this is your dad, but you should know he is supposed to be in the jail right now."

"With Grandpa? Is he a policeman like Grandpa?"

"No, he's not a policeman. He ... "

"Shut up!" Barry yelled.

"Don't yell at my mom!" Zach yelled back. His eyes widened in confusion.

I pushed Zach behind me. My hands shook as I punched in 911 on my phone. The evening dispatcher, Manny Gomez ,answered. "Manny, this is Betsy. Barry is here."

"They're already on the way. They lost him when they took him to Benny's for supper."

I couldn't believe they had taken Barry out of jail to go get barbecue. Life in small-town Texas.

"Listen, son. I've been out working while I've been away. I've been working for you. I'm getting married again, and we'll have a room just for you. We need to get to know each other, son."

"Get out of here!" I yelled.

Barry walked toward us, and I picked up the broom in the corner of the kitchen. "I said get out!" I yelled, holding the broom out as a weapon.

"What are you going to do, sweep me to death? Oh, and by the way, I heard all about your little troubles in the library. Doesn't look too good for you, sweetie, if the judge has to decide custody for Zach between a con man father or a murdering mother...I think I win."

I pushed at him with the broom. He took hold of it with his hand and threw it behind him. "Now give me my son, dammit." He reached out and backhanded me. A sudden pain hit my jaw. I fell against the refrigerator and hit the floor. Zach screamed and ran to the front the door of the house. He was trying desperately to open the chain lock on the door, but his little fingers couldn't make it work. He was screaming as his fingers failed around the metal chain.

"Time to go home, son."

I grabbed my cast-iron frying pan from the wall and ran after him. My arm swooped through the air. The weight of the pan felt like it would pull out my limb at the elbow, but I connected and knocked Barry in the back of the head. He stumbled to the ground.

"That's for leaving us, you jerk," I said, standing over him. George Beckman came running in behind me and grabbed Barry by the arms. Barry was holding his head as the blood seeped between his fingers.

"You hit me, you sniveling bitch. Where did you get that from? Yeah, well you weren't worth staying for. You and your idiot son."

Zach ran to my arms, crying and saying my name over and over again.

George started walking Barry to the door. "We'll get you to the emergency room. Miss Betsy has quite a wild swing there when she needs it."

Oh great, wait until Chief Wilson heard about this. I had just done what I was accused of doing at the library, except Barry lived through it. I'm sure the comparison would be drawn between the two crimes.

"Why did that have to be my daddy, Mom? Why? He wasn't nice at all, and he hit you."

"It's okay, baby. It's okay."

Zach held me tight in his little arms. "Don't let him get me, Mom. Don't let him take me."

*****

Later as I soaked in a hot tub, I thought at least now they had some real charges against Barry. Breaking and entering, attempted abduction of a child and whatever else my dad would think of. Before my bath I sat with Zach until he fell asleep, his homework untouched. I tried to sort out all that had happened over the last couple of weeks. This all started with that darn crocodile cake. Sometimes you just have to come to the conclusion that baking leads nowhere but trouble. The smell of the lavender bath salts drifted through the air as I scrunched down in the tub, letting the warmth of the water seep through me.

Why did someone want to kill Vanessa? Everybody disliked the woman, that was true, but someone must have truly hated her to go that far. Maybe it was some random serial killer who had crept into the library to check the newest Curious George books. No, that wasn't it.

Okay, whoever killed her had to get past the library staff and into the partitioned-off children's section that was closed for painting. I knew that the painters left sometime in the afternoon, so they had to have come in after that. People came in for the meeting at 6:30, so the murder had to have occurred in that time frame. Who was available during that time? Probably everyone who came to the meeting that night. Even the dead Martha Hoffman was around. Of course, even though Martha was dead, that didn't mean she didn't kill Vanessa and then was killed herself by the random serial killer.

I took a deep breath from the steam rising up off the water. There were too many what-ifs in this murder. What if it was Edith out of jealousy? What if it was Damien because of her rejection of him? What if I can't figure it out and end up going to jail for a crime I didn't commit?

I was about to put my head under the water when my cell phone rang. I jumped out of the tub and grabbed a towel.

"Betsy?"

"Hi, Leo."

"Did I disturb you?"

"No, just taking a bath."

"Oh, uh you want me to call back?"

"No. Listen, I'm probably going to have to postpone our weekend for a few weeks."

"Really, that's good to know," he said. "We are about to open hurricane season here, and it looks like this is going to be a busy one. We already have one system in the Gulf, although it's too early for it to really turn into something at this point. We will be charting away on this one, though. Pretty exciting stuff. What's going on with you?"

"Oh, not much," I lied. "I just needed to put off our weekend because I'm still dealing with all of the fallout with finding Vanessa Markham dead."

"Oh yeah, what's happening now?"

I decided to tell him the latest. Better he know now I'd been accused of two murders than later when he visits me in the women's prison.

"Betsy, explain to me just how it is you get yourself so embroiled in these messes?"

"I didn't get myself into this on purpose, you know." This was starting to get me a little angry. Like I would purposely get myself accused of murder?

"I didn't mean it that way. I'm sorry, it's just that ... "

"I know. Oh, and one other thing. Barry showed up, and I knocked him in the head with a frying pan." Silence on the other end.

"Did you ... kill him?

"No, it seems when I really do try to kill someone, I'm not so good at it," I said. "He was trying to take Zach from me. I couldn't let that happen."

"Is there anything I can do to help?"

"I guess just taking a rain check right now is the best you can do."

"Absolutely – and remember that means we are going to have our weekend just as soon as you dodge that murder charge, and, um, possible assault charge."

"And you dodge that hurricane."

"At least we're not boring people," he said

"I wish we were," I replied. "At least we'd be together."

CHAPTER 25

I drove over to Andersonville the next morning, resolved to get to the bottom of all of this. Rocky had called to see if he could interview me as a person of interest for the Pecan Bayou Gazette. I told him by the time our weekly paper comes out, the police would have somebody else for a suspect. Rocky laughed, but deep down I wondered if he believed me. At least he now had Edith's address given to him by Peter so he could send over his last paycheck.

The temperature was rising just a little bit from the week before. Sometimes I felt like the heat creeping in degree by degree was just our way of paying the rent for the incredible springs we were blessed with. In South Texas, spring starts in mid-February and lasts all the way until May. I rolled down my windows, smelling the sweet nectar of the spring flowers, and turned up the radio. I hated to slow down as I neared the fairgrounds on the edge of Andersonville. This town was a little bit bigger than Pecan Bayou, sporting four stoplights instead of our two.

They also had a bigger paper. The Andersonville Register had already hired Peter to cover sports and whatever else they needed him for. It was located on the main street, so I decided to start there and then try to talk to Edith. She wasn't exactly my biggest fan, and me showing up to talk to Peter would undoubtedly make her jealous all over again.

The Andersonville Register was situated in a large gray stucco building on a corner across from the town supermarket. Peter's car, a red Camaro, was parked out front.

"Betsy?" I heard my name as I entered the front office of the Register. I turned, and Peter was sitting behind his desk, much the same as I had seen him day after day in the offices of the Gazette. He had been leaning back, balancing on the back two legs of his chair, chewing on the edges of a pencil. He looked much better than he had at our last meeting, now clean-shaven, showered and looking like the GQ model he should have been.

"What are you doing here?" he asked, getting up from his chair to extend his hand and then returning to it as I pulled up my own chair.

"I needed to talk to you about something."

"You, uh, could have called."

"I know, but I also needed to discuss this with Edith as well."

Peter gestured me into the newsroom behind a swinging half door. "Did you hear about Martha Hoffman?" I asked.

"No, but I did have a message to call a Sergeant George Beckman this morning from the Pecan Bayou Police Department," he said. "Is she the person who killed Vanessa? I hadn't had a chance to call. To tell you the truth, it's awfully nice to be away from all of that."

"I know. I wouldn't mind being away from it, too. Martha Hoffman was found dead."

"Seriously?" Peter's chair wheels squeaked on the tile floor.

"Pretty serious. Someone strangled her with the belt from her robe."

"When?"

"I guess it was night before last. They said she probably knew who her killer was, but here's the thing – they found a note that was typed up and signed by me saying I was going to kill her."

"Did you write her a note like that?"

"No. That's why I'm here," I said. "I need to find out where everyone who was at Vanessa's murder was during Martha's murder."

"You mean like an alibi?" Peter laughed. "Okay, another alibi for the police over there. Let's see, I guess I was home alone that night because Edith was out doing a book talk at the Texas Sweethearts Romance Readers Club. That gives you her alibi too, so you won't have to track her down – and trust me, you don't want to have to track her down. You wouldn't believe the grief she gave me seeing you hugging me at my front door."

"Good to know," I said. "I appreciate that, Peter. I'll check with the people at the romance novel club to corroborate Edith, but how about you?"

"No can do. I was watching a baseball game on television. That's all there was too it. I went to bed before the game even finished. Since Vanessa's death, I seem to be sleepy all the time."

"Well, that's what the police are probably calling about."

"Have you ever thought of the possibility that the two murders are not connected?" he asked.

"Not really," I replied. "Both women were involved in the author night. They have to be connected."

"Maybe Martha finally stamped somebody's library card the wrong way," he said.

"You mean like mine?

"Yours and half the town's. I was in there one day trying to check out something in an old Sports Illustrated, and she was telling off some little kid for bending a page.

She wasn't exactly Mother Goose."

CHAPTER 26

Later that day when I walked into the children's section of the Pecan Bayou Library, Peter's words echoed in my head. Maybe the two murders weren't connected, but somehow I felt I had to piece together the first murder in order to get whoever did the second one.

"Can I help you?" I turned around to see a pleasant young woman dressed in a pink short-sleeved blouse and gray skirt. "Yes ... um ... no. I was just looking around. The place looks a lot better than the last time I was here. I should probably tell you I'm the person who discovered Vanessa Markham's body on the floor there." I pointed to the freshly replaced carpet.

"Oh," she said in recognition. "That must have been awful for you." What a marked contrast she was to Martha Hoffman. Maybe the library job bitters you after a few years, but this girl was delightful.

"I was just wanting to look around for a bit."

"Oh," she repeated. "No problem. Take as much time as you would like."

"Let me ask you," I said, "do you know exactly what time the painters left that day?"

"Um, I heard it was around 4:30 or 5," she said. "I could get you the name of the painting contractor, if you would like."

"That would be great, thank you," I answered as I followed her back to the checkout desk.

"I usually work on the weekends so I wasn't here that day," she said. "After Martha was ... found ... my schedule was changed to full-time, so now I'm here during the week."

"Congratulations ... sort of."

"I know. It doesn't seem right. Martha put her heart and soul into this library, and even though I wanted her job, I sure didn't want it this

147

way." She wrote down the name of the painter on a small piece of paper and handed it to me. "Anyway, I hope you find what you're looking for."

I walked back over to the children's reading area and positioned myself to stand where she was when she fell. If someone came in through the accordion doors, everyone in the library must have seen them. Could the person have been hiding somewhere in the room, and if they were, how did they get into the room in order to hide after the painters left? There had been a wet paint sign on an easel that I remembered having to step around. It would have noticeable from Martha's perch at the checkout desk. Maybe the person slipped in when Martha was telling off some little kid for bending down the corner of a page?

I glanced around the room looking for a place to hide. The bookshelves were all waist-high so the killer would have to have scrunched down behind one of them. In one corner was a giant cardboard grandfather clock. I walked over to it and pulled it away from the wall. The backside of the clock revealed an open cavity that could have easily housed a person who was hiding. I put the cardboard clock back against its resting place. The seven-foot-high monster from *Where the Wild Things Are* filled up the other corner. He was big enough and wide enough that someone could have easily hidden behind him. I walked over and slid him out a bit to see how easy it was to hide. As I moved the giant stuffed creature, I discovered how the killer got past the librarian. The monster was blocking another door.

The killer could have used that door to sneak in and then sneak back out again. The door had a sticker on it claiming an alarm would sound if the door was opened. I could understand why they would put the enormous stuffed monster over there to discourage little ones from trying the door and ending up in the library parking lot.

Knowing I would probably get myself in trouble but at this point not really caring, I tried opening the door. As I pushed on the metal bar, the door opened out to the side of the grassy lot the library stood on. Where was the alarm? I took in a deep breath and waited for sirens in my ears. After about twenty seconds of silence, it seemed there were to be none. I let the door close behind me and then tried to reopen it. It was locked. So I knew how the killer got out, but I wasn't sure how he or she might have entered. As I walked back around to the front of the library, I pulled my cell phone out of my purse and called my dad.

"Did you know there's a door to the outside in the children's section of the library?"

"Yes, but the library staff always tries to keep it blocked and there's an alarm on the thing."

"I have news for you," I said. "I just opened it and there is no alarm. Getting out was pretty easy."

I heard the squeak of his office chair at the police department, and I knew he was pulling up to his computer. "That changes things a bit."

"It sure does. It had to be used by the killer either to get in or out."

"Or both."

"The door is locked from the outside, but the room was being painted. What if the painters opened that door for ventilation while they were working there?" I suggested.

"The killer could have slipped in the open door and hidden."

"One problem, though."

"What's that?"

"How did Vanessa Markham get in?"

"Now that's a good question."

"Do you have the name of the painting contractor who was working in the children's section that day?" I asked.

"Sure." I heard a couple of papers shuffle. "It was Mid-Texas Painting."

"Were you the one who questioned them?"

"No. It was Arvin Wilson. I'm not allowed, remember?"

"I remember. I'm thinking about heading over there."

I heard a yawn on the other end. "Will you look at the time? Lunch already? I'll meet you there in twenty minutes."

*****

I didn't recognize the caller ID of my next call as I drove to the address the dispatch operator of Mid-Texas Painters told me to go to. Today they were painting a house over on Walnut Street.

"Miss Livingston? This is Damien Perez. I need to speak with you. Can you meet me somewhere?"

"Sure. What is this about?"

"I just need to speak with you, alone," he said.

"Okay, how about we meet at Earl's Coffee in about an hour and a half?"

I parked on the street beside a medium white panel truck with the sliding door in the up position. I could see the tools and cans lined up neatly inside the truck. The painters of Mid-Texas Painting were sprawled out on the lawn enjoying their fast-food lunches, some of them already napping in the shade of the tree. I walked up to the men, and one of them rose from the lawn and wiped his hands on his white-splattered coveralls.

"What can I do for you? Need something painted?" he said.

"Most likely, but I'm here about the job you did at the public library a week ago."

"Oh, that job. Are you sure this isn't police business?"

"I'm the one who discovered the body," I said. "I'm also the one that seems to be the main suspect in that killing and the death of the librarian just a day ago."

The painter looked at me and stood back a bit. He had to outweigh me by at least a hundred and fifty pounds, and yet he seemed nervous. "Really?"

I cut in. "I was wondering if you saw or heard anybody that day."

"I'll tell you just what I told the police. Didn't hear anybody and didn't see anybody."

"When you were painting, did you open the exit door?"

"Yeah, we had to," he said. "That old bat wouldn't let us open those folding doors, and we were going to die from the fumes in there. I wasn't supposed to, but I had to think of my men." The men sitting on the grass nodded in agreement.

"Did you ever leave the room and also leave the door open?"

"When we ate lunch," he said. "We went out to eat under the trees at the library." The trees he spoke of were about fifty feet from the door that had been propped open. Someone could have easily slipped in if the men were not looking directly at the door.

"Did your men maybe doze off under the trees?" said my dad, who had joined us.

"I think we all did that day. I had a terrible headache from the paint not being ventilated right," said the painter.

Now I knew how the killer got in – but what about the victim?

CHAPTER 27

An hour later, I sat at Earl's enjoying anything but a caramel macchiato. Possibly an iced coffee would keep me from from crashing my car into the local trees.

"Thank you for meeting me so quickly, Betsy." Today Damien Perez had on a black short-sleeved shirt and tan pants. He wore his sunglasses up in his pitch-black hair, and as he spoke, he fingered the gold watch on his arm.

"You must know I am quite distraught over Vanessa's murder."

"Of course."

"I am mourning, the same as Peter, even though Vanessa and I quarreled shortly before her murder."

I was confused. "I thought you broke up?"

"Yes, yes. We broke up, but that wasn't something I wanted. It was what she wanted. I was in love with her."

"If I may ask, what was the reason she gave to break up with you?"

He stretched out his arms and placed them behind his head as he seemed to be remembering their affair with great fondness. "I know, it is hard to believe. We had been so happy together. We were like a symphony together."

"But she wanted to end it?"

"Unbelievable. She said she had become bored with me. Me? I was greatly surprised by this."

I took another sip of my coffee, set it down and leaned toward him across the table. "So what did you want to share with me? Did you remember something that you forgot to tell me?"

"I found something. Quite by accident." He leaned over and took a cell phone out of his pocket. "I am terrible with this thing. My agent wants me to wear one of those earpieces so he can constantly be calling me." I had the feeling phones were like women for Damien Perez. He would be the one to decide when and where to use them. "I had to check on a text my publicist sent me for another of those dreary book signings. That is when I discovered it."

"What?"

"A text ... from Vanessa. She texted me a few hours before her murder."

Damien tapped the buttons on his smart phone until a text screen appeared.

> *I cannot see you. I have to deal with this woman. What she is doing is wrong and I can't let her get away with it.*

"You know her husband was having an affair with Edith Martin. Maybe she found out after the first author night," I said.

"I don't believe so," Damien replied. "I watched her that first night in hopes that she had changed her mind about us. Her eyes weren't on Edith. She didn't seem to notice her at all."

"What was she looking at?"

"She was watching two women. Martha Hoffman and ... you."

"Me? I know we had an argument that the entire mall seemed to have heard, but I didn't consider it all that serious. Did you think she did?"

"I don't know, but each time she would gaze down the table I was hoping it was my eyes she was trying to meet. It was not. She was looking past me at you."

I took a piece of paper out of my purse and wrote down the text. "Have you shared this with the police, Damien?"

He shrugged. "I haven't. You are in trouble, and I don't believe you are guilty. When I first read this, I must admit I thought she was talking about you."

I gulped. "I suppose it could have been me she was writing about, but our altercation ended that day... or at least I thought it did. That's why it has to be Edith."

"Of course." He closed his phone. "And I will go over to the police station directly and report this text."

"Good. I know it will help them and me – and thank you."

"For what?"

"For thinking of telling me first and believing in me."

He took my hand and gently kissed it. "De nada," he said softly.

*****

I ran over to the Gazette to ask Rocky if he knew whether Vanessa knew Edith was the other woman. Maybe Vanessa had said something to him or yelled it out in the office when she was scolding Peter. Rocky was behind his computer in the back when I entered.

"Betsy, this is a surprise. I'm glad you stopped by," he said. "I wanted to let you know I found another columnist to replace Vanessa. We now have an official gardening column that will start with next week's paper."

"That's great, Rocky. How's the new guy doing?"

"Oh, Tim? He's great when he's not texting on his phone. This generation is all about communicating without face time."

"That's what Facebook is for."

"Why do they call it that? That's what I'd like to know," said Rocky. "Do you ever actually see the other person's face? No. You see whatever face they want you to see. Whatever happened to the good old-fashioned 'Let's have coffee and I'll tell you what's going on in my life?'"

"Thing of the past, Rocky – but funny you should mention coffee. I just had a cup with Damien Perez, who showed me a text Vanessa sent before she died." I pulled out the scrap of paper I had written it on and showed it to him.

"Was she that angry at you?"

"I didn't think so. When I read this I thought it might be Edith Martin she was texting about," I said. "Did you ever hear her mention her name when she was in the office?"

Rocky cupped his elbow in his hand and leaned against the other. "I don't think she did. There was an awful lot of yellin' going on in here." He shook his head. "I just don't recall anything being said about a specific name. It was more like she was focused on the act she caught him in, not who he was doing the act with."

"Great," I said. "Damien Perez is about to report the text to the police. What's to say they won't immediately assume she was talking about me?"

"Did you ever stop to think she might have been talking about Martha Hoffman? It's out now that she wrote Vanessa's book."

"Oh my gosh, you're right. It had to have been Martha."

"Which is a theory that works great until you realize Martha is dead, too. Who killed her? Vanessa from the grave?"

I glanced at my watch. "Almost time for Zach to get home. Good luck with your gardening column. Who's writing it, by the way?"

"Ruby Green from The Best Little Hair House. Isn't Ruby Green just the best name for a gardener?"

"Are you going to put a green thumb next to her picture?"

He laughed. "Maybe I will."

CHAPTER 28

"Alright Danny, hand me one more." Zach slowly perched a tiny yellow Lego onto a fire-engine red duplicate. Danny and Maggie had come over for dinner and one more try at breaking a world record. He was going to stack as many Legos in a continuous line as he could on our dining room table. Zach loved these little plastic blocks and probably had well over a thousand of them. Probably one of the most painful things a parent faces in cleaning up toys is stepping on that one piece of hard, bone-crunching Lego that was missed.

Danny sat in a chair, holding the bucket ready to hand off the next Lego. Aunt Maggie and I sat in the next room watching television. Aunt Maggie loved reality TV, and tonight she was wrapped up in the show about the desert island. I watched the endless scenes of people talking to the camera about the other contestants but soon tuned out.

Who was Vanessa texting about? Was this the person who killed her? Could Peter Markham be living with his wife's killer, or had they been in it together? I had worked next to Peter for a couple of years now, and he never seemed like the type. Edith I didn't know all that well, but how could a woman who spent her days writing about love and passion use murder to solve a problem? Maybe she had passion in anger as well as love?

I glanced at the show, where scantily clad castaways were eating what looked like live bugs. It was amazing what people would do for a million dollars. Eating bugs in your underwear in front of a worldwide audience was a little much even for that kind of money.

"Mom!" I heard from the other room. "This is taking a long time. Could we have some soda?" Zach said. "Yeah," Danny chimed in.

"No, you can have some milk. Soda will keep you up all night." I rose to go get two glasses of milk when the phone rang.

"Miss Livingston? This is Xavier Frank. Sorry to call you so late. You told me if I remembered anything else to let you know? Well, I remembered something ... "

*****

I sat outside in the parking lot waiting for a killer. It was dark except for one street lamp about forty yards away. I could be wrong. I could be overreacting. Better yet, I could just forget about this and be home in my bed, asleep, waiting for the police department to come and arrest me for a murder I didn't commit.

A bat flew by the front windshield of my Uncle Jeeter's old truck. I saw the reflection of the glass door trip against the light as it opened and closed. It was time. I stepped out of the truck and leaned against it, folding my arms. I wasn't sure if I was trying to look cool or to protect myself from flying candelabras.

"Betsy? What are you doing out here?"

"Waiting for you."

"Did we ... did I miss something? I don't remember anything about us getting together tonight, but I'm glad to see you. Boy, what a day I had today."

"No, we didn't have anything planned. This is all kind of spur-of-the-moment."

"Okay. Are you feeling alright? You're acting kind of weird."

"I'm feeling fine," I said, "but then, I don't eat a lot of cupcakes, Pattie."

Pattie stopped. Her smile fell flat. "Betsy? What are you talking about?"

"I'm talking about your cupcakes and how the whole town loves them."

"Thank you," she said. "I work very hard."

"They love them so much you could almost say they're addicted to them."

Pattie laughed. "I know what you mean. I have some people who come in every single day for their cupcake fix."

"Including Vanessa Markham. Vanessa who took such good care of her appearance found herself all of a sudden unable to stop eating your delicious cupcakes."

"The prettier they are the harder they fall."

"Vanessa was so upset about it she actually had one of your cupcakes analyzed by a nutritionist down in Houston."

Pattie started fidgeting with the bag she had carried out of the bakery."Really? That's interesting. Do you know what came out of that?"

"Oh, you know ... flour, sugar ... and an addictive food additive," I said.

"What?"

"It's called bliss butter. It's an interesting concoction that's made by mixing butter, sugar and a few extra chemicals that serve to increase the hunger-producing hormone, ghrelin. Combine this with the refined carbohydrates that cupcakes already have, and wham! You have yourself a money-maker. The delicious mixture of the flour, sugar and regular butter makes people feel blissful, but when you add just that little extra kick, your cupcakes are to die for."

"I'm sorry to hear you put it that way." Pattie pulled a long cake knife with a serrated edge out of her bag and lunged for me. I jumped back, narrowly avoiding the blade.

"Wait!" I said. "Before you kill me, I think I deserve to know some answers. How did you end up killing Vanessa in the library? There were people everywhere who would have seen you."

Pattie was breathing hard but edging up on me with the knife. "Don't you get it? People don't look at me. I'm the girl who serves the food. I slipped in when the painters left the door open and then waited. The fumes from the paint made my head hurt, but I hid behind that cardboard clock. Vanessa had it all figured out and threatened to reveal what I was doing if I didn't pay her off. I told Vanessa to meet me there before the meeting and I would give her the money she asked for. She showed up a half hour before the meeting and unbelievably just walked past the sign and no one stopped her. Martha was back in the meeting room setting up chairs, so it was perfect for me. Once she was in the door, I dragged her to the back and hit her with the candlestick. The whole thing only took about two minutes' time. I ran out the back door, closed it and went to my van to change. Easy to kill her – easier than I ever thought it would be. Killing you will be a little more difficult." She laughed. "How am I ever going to pin it on you? We didn't even have an argument in public."

Pattie stepped forward and began to raise the knife. I jockeyed out of the way and put my hand up again. "Did you kill Martha, too?"

"Yes, I killed her in order to make the police think it was you. Pretty clever about the note, huh? I just took it off of your charge slip for Danny's birthday cake. Oh, and don't worry. The cake was straight. Nothing in it."

"What a comfort to know you refuse to drug kids."

Pattie smiled and nodded, but then, as if remembering her purpose, she ran up on me and raised the knife when car lights went on all over the parking lot. I put my hands up and backed away from her.

My dad and Chief Wilson grabbed Pattie by the shoulders and pulled her away from me. She shrieked and kicked as they tried to get control of the hand with the knife in it.

"I trusted you! How could you betray me like this!"

My dad put handcuffs on Pattie. "Need anything else, there, Chief?"

"That ought to do it, Judd," said Arvin Wilson. "Good job, Betsy. We appreciate your help in this matter. We got everything on tape from the wire you're wearing."

I slowly slid down the side of the truck, catching my breath. "I would never have believed it."

"Believe it!" Pattie yelled. "That bitch found out about my secret ingredient and was going to let the whole world know if I didn't cut her in. She never had to work for anything in her life. I get up at dawn and start baking and don't quit until after supper. I'm workin' my ass off and she's going to come in and take my money?"

"Where did you get the idea to create the bliss butter?" I asked.

"I may have only been to junior college, but I know food," said Pattie. "I read up on it and then discovered I could get what I needed off the internet. Like you said, it didn't take a lot, just enough to make people feel happy."

"I can't believe you, Pattie," I said. "I thought you were my friend."

Pattie looked down at the dark parking lot. "I *was* your friend. I mean, I liked you and all, but when the thing happened at the mall and Vanessa got so angry, you just became the natural course of action. Everyone would believe you did it because she insulted your kid. It just kind of fell into my lap, so lose a friend and keep my business."

My father started escorting her to the waiting patrol car. "Don't worry, Pattie," he said, "you'll meet all kinds of new friends in jail. If they let you cook in the prison bakery, the inmates will never have had it so good."

"You think they might?" Pattie asked.

"I'll put in a good word for ya."

*****

"And so this is Betsy Livingston, The Happy Hinter, hoping you learned a little something today. Thank you." The scene on the television dimmed as I clicked the TV off with the remote. I snuggled on the couch next to Leo Fitzpatrick. "Thanks, Leo. I had no idea you had been a TV weatherman for a while. All of your tips about relaxing in front of the camera really helped."

"And letting you film on location and out of the studio. The best hurricane coverage is the guy standing in the rain," he said. "I'm just glad you finally made it to Dallas, Betsy."

"It was touch-and-go there for awhile."

"Yeah, we could be having this conversation through protective glass, I guess."

"It was looking that way," I said. "If I hadn't gotten that call from Xavier Frank, I never would have known. I wouldn't have even suspected her of anything. She was always so nice to me. I'm actually going to miss her."

"Don't you mean you're going to miss her cupcakes? The whole town must be going through withdrawals right now," he said. "An entire town with the munchies, what a story."

"I really only ate one or two of her cupcakes, and they were dreamy, but with my lack of baking skills I guess I never really developed too much of a sweet tooth. Vanessa, on the other hand, had boxes hidden everywhere."

"Which, for someone who was conscious of her weight and appearance, probably made her feel the same guilt an overeater would feel."

"Yes, she was feeling like the same people she had probably been insulting for all of her life. Kind of ironic, isn't it?"

"So Peter goes off to live happily ever after with Edith ..."

"Update on that story," I said. "Now that he has the other woman, he's decided it's really not so exciting for him."

"Really?"

"I guess when you don't have to sneak around anymore, the thrill is gone. But from what I saw of Edith, she'll survive."

"She always has her writing."

"I'll say."

Leo leaned over and kissed me on the curve of my neck. I continued, trying to ignore him. "And then there's Oscar Larry. He was caught doctoring up a photo using pie plates hanging from a string. The UFO followers would have fallen for it if they hadn't seen the Mrs. Jones Baked Pies logo on the bottom of the saucer."

"Another person ruined by baking."

I laughed. "I guess so."

"And what happened to the vampire guy?"

"Damien Perez? I don't know. The last I heard, he was looking into writing about Mexican werewolves in Texas or the chupacabra. Gee, maybe he could write a book about a vampire and a werewolf both falling in love with a young girl?"

"Sounds familiar," Leo said. "So those are all the reasons you kept having to put off our weekend?"

I took a sip of my wine. "Oh, and one more. Zach was trying to break a world record with his cousin Danny."

"And did he succeed?"

"Only if there's a world record for the number of failed attempts to break a world record."

Fitzpatrick laughed and stirred the logs on the fire. He turned back to me and took me into his arms and began to kiss away all of the tension, worry and fears of the last month. I felt myself sinking into the moment ... Then my phone jangled in my pocket, making us both jump.

"Mom? I was wondering, do you have any matches?" Zach was still at it. "Danny and I are going to break the world record for lighted candles. Don't worry, we won't wake up Aunt Maggie. She's been snoring for the last hour ... "

Hints From the Happy Hinter

How to Plunge a Sink or Tub

Most minor sink clogs can be cleared with a plunger. Partially fill the sink with water, then start plunging. Vigorously work the plunger up and down several times before quickly pulling it off the drain opening. If it's a double-bowl kitchen sink, stuff a wet rag into one drain opening while you plunge the other one. If it's a bathroom sink, stuff the rag into the overflow hole. This helps to put pressure directly on the clog.

Recycling Freezer Containers

When freezing food in gallon-sized bags, trying storing the bags in recycled cake mix and cereal boxes. Make sure you label the front of the box and the bag itself so you don't forget what you put into it. Also, put a "use by" date on your label. Here's a guide for the freezer life of various foods:

Fruits and vegetables: homegrown, 12 months; store-bought, 8 months

Muffins, biscuits: 2-3 months

Loaves, doughnuts, rolls: 1-2 months

Baked cakes: 4-6 months

Cupcakes and baked pies: 2-3 months

Cookies: 8-10 months

Cookie dough: 6 months

Roast beef, steaks: 6-9 months

Ground beef or cubes: 2-3 months

Beef stew: 6 months

Pork roast: 3-6 months

Pork chops/ribs: 2-3 months

Chicken: 10 months

Turkey or duck: 6 months

Lean fish: 6 months

Fatty fish: 2-3 months

Shellfish: 6 months

Cake Baking Tips

1. To cut an unfrosted cake in half, use a taut string or dental floss to do the job.

2. When decorating a cake with frosting, clip off the end of a sandwich or storage bag and fill it with icing. If you were using a tubed icing with a decorator tip, try using that tip with the baggie.

3. If you need to make black frosting, try adding blue food coloring to chocolate icing.

4.Using a lazy susan or turntable will make the frosting process easier because you can always have the part you are working on in front of you.

5. Level off any bumps or rises in your cakes with a serrated knife to have a more uniform cake for frosting.

6. Listen to Pattie and don't overcook the cake. Moist is better.

Betsy's Tater-Tot Casserole

2 lbs ground meat (beef or turkey)

2 cans cream of mushroom soup

1 cup water

2 cups grated cheddar cheese

1 bag frozen tater tots

Brown ground meat and drain. Place in casserole dish. Combine soup and water; pour over meat. Sprinkle cheese over soup. Top with tater tots. Bake at 350 for 1 hour. Serve hot. This recipe can be made lower fat by using fat-free cream of mushroom soup, ground turkey and fat-free cheddar cheese.

Coffee Creamer Recipes

Liquid Coffee Creamer
Basic Recipe:

1 14 oz. can sweetened condensed milk
1 1/2 cups milk

Lowfat Version:

1 14 oz. can lowfat sweetened condensed milk
1 1/2 cups skim milk

Powdered Coffee Creamer
Unflavored powdered coffee creamer
A bottle of your favorite coffee syrup
Boil 2 cups water, remove from burner, add 1 cup powdered creamer, mix, add flavored syrup to taste. Store in covered container in refrigerator.

The Magic of Dryer Sheets
Use a dryer sheet to dust your baseboards. Because of the coating on the dryer sheet, your baseboards will repel dust and pet hair better. You can also put your dryer sheet on your Swiffer mop to grab all the pet hair and dust off your floors.

Get Rid of Moths Without Mothballs
Make a small drawstring bag out of cotton or cheesecloth. Fill the bag with this mixture:
1 part dried lavender
1 part rosemary
1/2 part dried lemon peel
1 Tablespoon cloves
Fill the bag about half full and hang it in your closet. Scrunch the bag from time to time to release its scent. When the bag loses its scent, discard the herbs and refill it with fresh ingredients.

About the Author

Teresa Trent writes cozy mysteries that take place in small towns in Texas. She was born in Chattanooga, Tennessee but with her father in the military, didn't stay for long. She's lived all over but has a special place in her heart for Colorado, Illinois and of course, Texas. Being a fan of the Andy Griffith Show and Murder She Wrote she loves creating quirky small towns and colorful characters. She decided to feature a character with Down syndrome in the Pecan Bayou series because after giving birth to her son with DS, she discovered there were very few people like him in the world of cozy mysteries. She continues that with the character of Gigi, a young woman with cerebral palsy in the Henry Park Series. Teresa lives in Houston, Texas with her husband, two of her adult children and a needy dachshund mix named Martin Luther.

Series By Teresa Trent

The Pecan Bayou Series
#1 A Dash of Murder
#2 Overdue for Murder
#3 Doggone Dead
#4 Buzzkill
#5 Burnout
#6 Murder for a Rainy Day
#7 Till Dirt Do Us Part
The Henry Park Series
#1 Color Me Dead

Don't miss out!

Visit the website below and you can sign up to receive emails whenever Teresa Trent publishes a new book. There's no charge and no obligation.

https://books2read.com/r/B-A-FJQD-JRDO

BOOKS 2 READ

Connecting independent readers to independent writers.

Also by Teresa Trent

Henry Park
Color Me Dead

Pecan Bayou
A Dash of Murder
Overdue for Murder
Doggone Dead
Buzzkill
Burnout
Murder for a Rainy Day
Till Dirt Do Us Part
Oh Holy Fright
Die a Yellow Ribbon

Redbird Creek
The Con Man's Daughter

Watch for more at https://teresatrent.com.